Python's Embrace

Bitten Point, #3

Eve Langlais

Copyright and Disclaimer

Published by Eve Langlais
1606 Main Street, PO Box 151
Stittsville, Ontario, Canada, K2S1A3
http://www.EveLanglais.com

ISBN-13: 978-1522802273
ISBN-10: 1522802274

Chapter One

Stupid swamp. The water had long ago leeched all the warmth from her limbs. Worse, though, was the mud. It sucked at Aria's limbs when she tried to rest. It coated her in a slimy second skin that reeked so badly even the bugs didn't dare make a feast out of her. But at least it hid her from the trackers.

Despite the fatigue drugging all her senses, she knew they were out there, searching. Hunting…

Hunting for me so they can drag me back to the institute and silence me forever—or worse.

Never.

Capture wasn't an option. Since her escape, she hadn't stopped running. She'd swum until her arms threatened to fall off. Slogged through thick marsh until her legs filled with heavy lead. She wanted to lie down and take a long nap, but that would mean giving up, and that wasn't an option.

The monsters at Bittech hunted her, and she didn't mean just Merrill and his henchmen. Real monsters existed. Beasts without conscience. They would just as soon find her as kill her. Nowhere was safe, not land, air, or water.

But I refuse to be their next victim. She wouldn't give in without a fight.

An ululating shriek came in the distance, an

eerie sound that echoed, silencing the normal creatures that roamed the night. Stillness descended as even the bugs stopped their hum, and her breath froze in her lungs.

They unleashed the aerial hunters. She'd hoped to clear the swamp before that happened. Hell, she'd hoped to make it out of Bitten Point before nightfall. However, the bayou hadn't cooperated, and now that full dark had arrived, the chase was truly on.

As the primal scream filled the dark sky again, she didn't move for a moment, just remained crouched in the mud and weeds, hoping against hope the hunter wouldn't spot her. She couldn't help but crane to peer at the sky overhead, dark yet glittering with thousands of stars.

For a moment, a shadow appeared, spotlighted against the moon, a rapier-gazed creature aloft on leathery wings.

Did it see her? Would it dive? She ducked down lest the whites of her eyes give her away. She lay huddled, still and barely breathing.

Shrieking in annoyance, the hunter banked and flapped away.

A few dozen heartbeats later, she dared to suck in a lungful of air and face forward, only to blink at her newest predicament.

Grrr.

The vicious sound came from a beady-eyed creature, its furry muzzle curled back to reveal tiny pointed teeth.

Grrr.

Did it seriously think to threaten her? She'd eaten squirrels bigger than that for snacks.

But of more concern than the aggressive appetizer was the shadow that rose above them both. A deep voice said, "Well, well, Princess, what do we have here?"

"Trouble if you don't get out of my way." Aria glared at the big dude through a dirty hank of hair. Even she could admit she lacked an intimidation factor, yet when he dared to laugh, she didn't think twice before acting.

The handful of mud hit the behemoth square in the face with a satisfying splat.

"Did you really just do that?" he asked with clear annoyance as he wiped the mud from his face with a hand.

Dumb question seeing as how she had. "Get out of my way."

"Or what?"

Perhaps flinging a second handful wasn't the most mature response. Her excuse? *I'm tired.*

Before she could explain how he deserved it, Princess attacked!

The tiny dog soared over Aria's shoulder, and she swiveled her head to watch as the little runt latched its teeth on the coral snake lying on the rock beside Aria. Princess shook her head viciously, not releasing her latch while the serpent hissed and spat its displeasure.

The incongruous sight made Aria blink, but it didn't change the scene. The tiny dog still held on, and the snake's spastic death thrash slowed.

Aria fluttered her lashes again as a large hand waved in front of her eyes.

"Let me help you out of the mud." The low rumble had her turning to peek up, way up, at the speaker.

In the gloom, she couldn't tell much about the dude other than he was big, really freaking big, and unconcerned that the little dog had viciously taken on a poisonous snake.

"Shouldn't you be helping your mutt?"

He snorted. "Princess would be offended if I butted in. She's more than capable of taking care of herself."

Sounded familiar. Aria also had an independent streak, and that meant she eschewed his offer of a hand to crawl out of the muck—because it was so much more impressive when she slogged through the sucking mud and crawled onto the scrub grass.

But she did it, just like she'd escaped Merrill and Harold and all the others hunting her.

Exhausted, Aria flopped onto her back, probably not her wisest course of action, especially since she didn't know the intentions of the big guy. For all she knew, he was some hillbilly psychopath who'd played a role in the making of the movie *The Hills Have Eyes*—stupid Cynthia making her watch it. Good news, she didn't hear a banjo. And really, how dangerous could a guy be who called a tiny mutt Princess?

Her gut didn't twinge. Her inner eagle didn't caw or flutter her feathers aggressively. Trusting her instincts, Aria remained lying on the ground, giving her tired body a needed moment of respite.

Given the big dude surely didn't see women crawling out of the swamp every day, she expected a barrage of questions. Normal people would ask things like, "What are you doing out here?" or, "How long do you intend to live?" Men with tempers didn't take kindly to women slinging mud in their faces.

The stranger, however, didn't say a word, but he did strip his shirt off and use it to mop his face. The shadows didn't allow her a clear view, but she saw enough to realize his bulk was comprised of muscle, not fat. Lots of muscle.

We should stroke it and soothe his ruffled feathers, her eagle suggested.

There would be no stroking. Aria looked away and noted his dog had finished with the snake. The poisonous serpent lay limp on the rock, and Princess pranced and yipped, celebrating her kill.

"What a good girl. Did Daddy's princess kill the nasty viper?"

Had the big guy seriously just baby-talked to his dog?

Rolling onto an elbow, she gaped at them.

The guy had crouched down to grab his little pet and held her cradled in the crook of one arm. The darned thing was barely a bite, yet the big dude, who smelled slightly reptilian himself, toted Princess as if she were made of fine spun glass while Aria lay in the dirt, looking and smelling like a pile of refuse.

So unfair. Although why she cared she

couldn't have said. *What does it matter if he mollycoddles his dog? And who cares if I'm filthy? I'm not looking to impress him.*

We need a bath, her avian side complained. While she could handle a little dirt, her inner eagle cringed at the filth coating them. Birds did not like filming their bodies with mud. It impeded their ability to fly.

Speaking of flying, time to get out of the swamp. She'd already spent too much time lying there and needed to get moving before the hunter made another pass.

Aria sprang to her feet, but moved too fast. Her vision wavered, as did her body. A hand steadied her.

"Careful there. I wouldn't want you to face-plant out here."

"Let me guess, you've got a softer spot for me to plant myself on? Like your bed or the backseat of your car?" She'd heard all the come-on lines, and none of them impressed her.

"Uh, no. What I meant was Princess does her business in this area. It's why we're out here, as a matter of fact. She had to do her business."

Squish. Aria's toes squeezed the warm piece of poop, and she couldn't help the hysterical giggle that bubbled from her. "Shit."

Chapter Two

What to make of the woman who'd just crawled from the bayou wearing only a bra and panties? In all his years, this was the first time such a thing had happened, at least to Constantine.

As he cradled Princess against his body, he couldn't help but catalogue the enigma standing before him.

What a tiny thing, not even close to his chin, and slim too. A layer of muck covered her. He couldn't smell if she was human or shifter, but by the way she moved, he would have wagered shifter—an animal with grace, given her fluid movements.

Questions brimmed on his lips, the foremost being, *who are you?* Yet, he held off. He sensed a certain skittish quality about her. It wouldn't take much to send her fleeing.

She can't run if we hug her. Squeeze her. Hold her tight.

His inner snake only ever had one solution for everything.

Perhaps instead of crushing her to death, we should try cleaning her up and getting some answers.

Because he'd wager her story had a lot to do with what he, his brother, and friends had been investigating over the past while.

Something hunted the people of Bitten Point. Something screwed with them, and it was past time they screwed back.

Or screwed her.

Bad snake, and he didn't mean his shifter one. A certain part of him showed a little too much interest in the mud-coated woman in front of him. How perverse to lust after a swamp creature, especially one who'd stepped in poop and possessed a very dirty mouth.

Very dirty…

He interrupted her litany of curses. "Listen, my place isn't far from here. I've got an outdoor shower if you'd like to sluice off."

The mud-spattered face peeked at him with suspicion. "I am not getting naked for your entertainment."

"Keep your clothes on then while you shower, see if I care, but you might find them uncomfortable, and it will be harder to rinse your, um, girly bits." Not usually a shy man, Constantine balked at mentioning her more feminine parts, especially since he found himself more interested in them than was normal.

"Don't you worry about my girly bits. As for stripping, exactly what am I supposed to wear after my shower? And if you say you, I will probably hurt you."

The threat drew a chuckle from him. A tiny lady, but feisty. He liked that. "I've got some spare clothes you can borrow so you don't have to parade around in your undergarments or the buff."

Her arms crossed over her chest, hiding her petite assets. "How do I know I can trust you?"

"Lady, I don't know what kinds of guys you associate with, but I can assure you I have no interest in ogling or molesting someone barely bigger than my dog. I prefer my ladies with more meat."

The words were meant as reassuring, yet her eyes flashed. "There is nothing wrong with being petite and fine-boned."

"It is if you want something to chew on." Constantine heard her suck in a breath and could have groaned. *I did not just say that.* But he had. Odd, because he wasn't usually one to talk crude to the ladies.

Given arguing in the swamp wouldn't get them anywhere, he turned on his heel. Despite the darkness, he didn't have any problems finding his way. He'd lived by the bayou for as long as he could remember. And he could remember a long time. Just about the only thing in his life he didn't recall was his daddy. That cold-hearted snake had left as soon as Constantine's mother announced her pregnancy, and the asshole had never come back.

But as his mommy said in his father's defense, it was in a snake's nature to leave once he'd fertilized a female.

Constantine's retort when he got old enough to reply, "Real men don't run from their responsibilities."

Words he meant, and yet, the fear he'd turn out like his father made him shy from relationships. *I don't want to be my father.* Already a python shifter by nature, he didn't want to add "lowdown bastard who ditched those who needed him" to that description.

As he strode from the edge of the marsh, dog tucked under his arm, he didn't bother to peek and see if the woman followed. Princess watched for him. Her little head turned to spy behind, her body tense in his grip.

It took only a few minutes of walking before the porch light appeared, a beacon in the darkness that drew all manners of flying bugs. This close to the Everglades, they saw their fair share of insects, some with enough legs and pinching mandibles to worry him. Princess had delicate skin.

A few more strides and the house he shared with his mother came into view. By most standards, it wasn't much. A compact, three-bedroom bungalow on wooden stilts. Heavy rains sometimes made the house appear as if it floated like an isle.

It chagrined him to realize he wondered what the woman thought of his home. *I'm not ashamed of where I come from.* Not ashamed, and yet, he kept pouring money into renovation projects. He also poured a lot of sweat and curse words.

The result? The house looked a lot more presentable than it used to. It had better seeing as how Constantine had spent plenty of his paychecks since he'd started working to improve the place. New siding, new windows, along with a roof he and Daryl, his older brother's best friend, had replaced themselves.

On the inside, he'd gutted the kitchen and put in new cabinets for his mom. Nothing fancy. He'd grabbed those prebuilt white ones on a clearance at the big box hardware store the next town over. But his mom loved it. Just like she loved the laminate flooring he'd installed throughout.

It might not seem like much, but it was home. *My home. Take it or leave it.*

Again, why he gave a shit, he couldn't have said. Besides, it wasn't as if she would be staying. He'd get her cleaned up and on her way as quickly as he could.

No leaving. Oursssss.

Not ours and, hell yeah, she was leaving. Constantine didn't run a home for muddy waifs. Even feisty ones that intrigued him.

He veered from the house as he hit the yard and headed to the outdoor shower unit. It didn't have much in the way of privacy, consisting of a single pole sticking up from the ground embedded in a concrete slab. The green garden hose, which he'd buried underground from the house to the outdoor unit, was clamped to the post and ended in a rusted showerhead at the top.

"There's the shower if you want to use it. I'll go grab you a towel. Ma keeps a pile of them stacked by the back door." Because, sometimes, Constantine liked to play in the mud, too.

The woman didn't reply. As a matter of fact, she'd not said a word at all. Whatever. He didn't pause to see if she turned on the water. Didn't care either if she stalked off. Less trouble for him if she did.

A squeak of a handle getting cranked and the

sound of rushing water let him know she'd stayed, but for how long?

The woman had yet to explain why she'd crawled out of the swamp, and while she didn't seem keen on his presence, she'd not taken off or demanded a phone.

Who was she?

Ourssss.

Despite his inner reptile's certainty, he was sure they had never met her before. Then again, given the coating of muck on her skin, she could have been his next-door neighbor for all he knew. Except old Kenny next door was about two hundred pounds heavier and a guy.

Still tucked under his arm, Princess wiggled, and he put her down on the ground beside him. His faithful companion stuck to his heels as he made his way to the mudroom at the back of the house he shared with his mom. And, no, he wasn't a mama's boy. Much.

However, he saw no reason to move out when his mother owned a perfectly sized house for them to share. He helped out with the bills and the man's work that needed doing while she cooked and washed his clothes. But it should be noted that he did do the dishes.

Within the mudroom, think plywood box on concrete patio stones, which basically acted as a shelter for the clothes washer and dryer, he snagged a clean towel with some vivid pattern. His ma long ago had given up on white linens. He and his brother were too dirty for it.

While in the mudroom, he also pulled open the dryer and scrounged out a long T-shirt, but he didn't bother with pants. He doubted she'd fit in his or his mother's. The woman he found possessed a waist so tiny he was sure both his hands could span it with room left over.

Someone needs to feed her.

I've got something to feed her.

Fuck, what the hell was wrong with him tonight? Ever since the fiasco in the tunnels a day or so ago, he'd found himself on edge. Jumping at shadows. Turning to check out every single noise. However, being vigilant didn't explain his odd interest in the muddy waif. Except she was probably not so muddy now.

I wonder what she looks like.

As he exited the mudroom, his gaze veered her way, and he noted she stood to the side of the outdoor shower, hand outstretched under the gushing torrent.

"It usually works better if you get under the spray," he remarked as he approached.

"It's cold."

"Well, duh. It's an outdoor shower. You didn't really expect us to pipe hot water out here."

The dirty look she tossed him from under a wet hank of hair almost made him smile.

"Hot water would have been nice."

"So would not tossing mud at people you meet for no reason. But I guess we both can't get what we want."

Her lips twitched. "Touché. Hypothermia it is

then."

"Once you get the mud off you, then we can get you into some warm stuff."

"What? Aren't you going to offer to warm me up yourself?" An impish tilt of her lips showed pearly white teeth. Teeth that he'd love to have nip him.

No, I don't. "I already told you, lady. You're not my type." Now someone tell that to his libido, which kept making sly remarks in his head.

"Good to know. Then I guess there's no need to tell you to turn your back while I strip off these rags."

The bra was first to go, and before he could avert his gaze, Constantine caught a glimpse of small peaches, tipped with hard buds, barely a mouthful. Yet so very tempting…

He quickly turned his head and heard her soft chuckle. "Prude."

"Most women would call it respect."

She snorted. "Now there's a word I don't hear often. Most men seem to think the fact I have a hole between my legs makes me fair game."

"Then I feel sorry for you because, in my world, women are to be cherished and protected."

"Must be nice."

Was it him, or did her words hold a wistful note? He didn't dare turn around to see, but he wanted to. Wanted to see the water cascading down her body, moisture pearling on the tips of her breasts.

Get a grip. He hung his head and closed his

eyes. He clenched his fists, too, as he breathed deeply, wondering at the strange effect she had on him.

Boring thoughts, such as the grass he needed to mow, helped him to somewhat resist her allure. The chatter of her teeth as she sluiced off under the spray also aided to bring him under control.

As soon as the water shut off, he held out the towel that dangled from his fist, still not daring to turn around.

She snagged it from him. "That was f-fucking cold," she stuttered.

I'll warm you up. He thought it, but said, "Are you decent?"

An unladylike sound emerged from her. "Not according to most of the people who know me."

"I meant are you wearing the towel?"

"Yeah, why?"

Pivoting on his heel, Constantine forgot what he meant to say as he saw her face. A face he recognized.

"Holy shit. You're Aria. The girl we've been looking for." The woman they'd combed the town for only to hit dead ends, literally. The body count kept growing.

The irony of her appearing practically at his doorstep would have made him laugh, except his snake chose that moment to hiss.

Finally, we have found the woman we've been waiting for.

Like hell.

Chapter Three

Damn and double damn. How did this guy recognize her?

"No, I'm not," she hastily replied. The last thing she needed was for word to get around that she'd escaped and surfaced. The crooked gang working in the underground lab at Bittech would come after her for sure if they found out. Better to let them think she'd died in the swamp.

As a matter of fact, she shouldn't let anyone know her whereabouts until she'd spoken to her boss and had gotten her ass to the safe house he'd told her to use in case things got hairy—or in this case, leathery.

The big guy snorted in reply to her rebuttal. "Of course it's you. I'm not a fucking idiot. Cynthia showed us enough pictures of you for me to know what you look like, especially now that your face is clean."

"You know Cynthia?"

"Damned straight I do. She hooked up with Daryl as soon as she came to town, and we've all been looking for you."

A moue twisted her lips. "Cynthia was supposed to go home and forget about looking for me." But she should have known her best friend wouldn't accept her disappearance.

"Don't be giving her shit because she cared."

A sigh left her. "I am not giving her hell, but her caring and coming to look for me complicated things. And how do you know Thea anyhow? Who are you?"

"Constantine Xavier Boudreaux."

She blinked. "Wow, that's a mouthful." Only too late did she realize how that sounded, and judging by the grin stretching his lips, so did he.

"More than a mouthful, and handful."

She couldn't help a roll of her eyes. "And there you go proving my point men only have one thought in their little brains."

"I thought we'd just ascertained mine was big." His smile widened.

A piercing shriek broke the staring match between them.

Immediately, she tensed and turned to look at the sky. "We need to get to cover."

"It's just some swamp bird looking for some dinner," the big man said as he leaned down to scoop his dog off the ground.

"I know. That's the problem. I think I might be his dinner." She muttered the last part, but he still heard.

"Don't worry. Whatever that is won't dare mess with us."

"Shows how little you know. And if you're not worried, then why are you picking up your dog?"

"Because she likes to be cuddled." He said it so seriously.

And she almost retorted, *I'd like to be cuddled,*

too. Except she didn't. Usually, that was.

Aria didn't like people touching her, but for some reason, she couldn't help but wonder what it would feel like to have this big guy put his hands on her.

Madness. Maybe a result of her time spent as a prisoner. *Am I going mad?*

Before she lost her mind, she needed to talk to her boss. "I need a phone." And a place out of the open. Despite Constantine's assurance that nothing would attack, he didn't know what she did.

The hunters weren't ordinary birds of prey, and while super-sized, Constantine wouldn't prove a match for those psycho beasts.

"Why don't you put this on first?" He thrust out a hand in which he gripped dark fabric. "I brought you a shirt."

"Is it a special shirt that I can use to dial someone's number?" was her sarcastic reply. She did, however, snatch it from him and tugged it over her head. Once it covered her, a yank on the towel pulled the damp cotton away from her body. "What should I do with this?" She waggled the wet towel.

"You can drop it in the laundry room."

"Which is where?" she asked.

"This way." Without any warning, he bent and forced her onto a wide shoulder before standing again.

Stung with shock, it took her a moment of dangling down his back before she yelled, "Put me down. What do you think you're doing?" Her shock at his actions explained her racing heart, but what she didn't understand was her eagle's lack of reaction. Where was the outrage? The anger?

A male should show his dominance.

Before she could digest that foreign concept, Constantine explained his illogic. "I am carrying you so your feet don't get muddy. And before you freak out some more, I might add I am doing the same thing with Princess."

"And this is the only way you thought to carry me?" she managed to say, not without a lot of incredulity.

"I only have one hand, lady. What else did you expect?"

"You could have put your dog down and carried me in both your arms."

A snort shook his frame. "Yeah, no. I'm not about to have my hands full and my dog vulnerable to whatever is in the sky."

As if to add weight to his argument, another screech pierced the night, closer this time. Aria couldn't help but shiver. While he might imagine the normal variety of hunter, she knew better. They needed to get out of the open.

She held her tongue, lest he change his mind about letting her use the phone. Another part of her, though, wondered at her blind trust of this behemoth.

This close, she could truly scent his skin. She'd spent enough time around shifters lately to realize he was a reptile of some kind. Kind being the key word.

"What are you?" she blurted out.

He didn't hesitate. "A snake. Python to be exact."

"I've never seen a snake shifter before."

"That's on account we're pretty rare. I got the gene from my dad. And you're one to talk about rare, seeing as how eagle shifters are just about extinct last I heard."

"How do you know what I am? I didn't realize snakes had such a good sense of smell." She answered her own question immediately. "Cynthia." Was there anything her best friend hadn't divulged?

Mental note to self: buy duct tape for her blabber- mouthed bestie.

"Were both your parents eagles?" he asked. A valid question since the same types of breeds had an easier time procreating.

"I don't know. I never knew them." Orphaned at a young age, Aria didn't just have no memories of her parents. She didn't have pictures or even names either. She knew nothing at all about who and what she was.

Coming into her shifter heritage as a teen had proved terrifying. The first burst of pain when she'd morphed for the first time sent her into a blind panic. It was a wonder she'd survived, given she crashed out of her bedroom window and tumbled to the ground, breaking an arm. She got in trouble for that, her foster parents not taking kindly to what they thought was a runaway attempt.

In a sense, they were right. She wanted to run...away from herself. For a few years, she thought herself a freak, a monster, until she met

Thea.

Actually, I crashed into her. She'd slammed Thea into a tree and exclaimed, "You smell different. You're like me. Except more doggyish."

Not the most auspicious of intros, and yet, from that moment, they became the best of friends.

It helped Aria to realize she wasn't alone. Thea was just like her, well, not exactly like, given Thea morphed into a wolf, but her friend knew about shifting. With her guidance and the lessons learned from Thea's parents, Aria came to understand what she was. She'd just never discovered who she was.

As they entered the house, another cry pierced the night, closer this time. Constantine shut the back door, shielding her from the eyes of the hunter. Or was that hunters? Merrill and his gang had more than one type of creature at their disposal. Would he dare unleash them all, though, in the hopes they'd bring her in—dead or alive?

Constantine crouched down, but if she thought he meant to put her down, she was mistaken. Only the dog got that privilege.

It seemed Princess didn't like her loss of status.

Yip.

"Sorry, Princess. Daddy's got to get Aria warm before she falls apart from shivering."

"I w-won't break." It might have sounded more convincing if she'd managed to say it without chattering teeth.

"No, but you might get sick. We need to get

you warm."

How about you just wrap me in those big arms of yours? He certainly felt awfully warm for a man who was supposedly cold-blooded.

She almost giggled. Then she frowned. What was wrong with her? Aria didn't cuddle. Nor did she want a man to hold her or warm her.

Dizziness assailed her as Constantine flipped her off his shoulder to cradle her in his arms. *Now who's the princess?* She bit her tongue before she could taunt the dog out loud.

"Let's get you to bed."

Bed with the big hunk?

"I'm not sleeping with you," she mumbled, barely managing coherence her shaking got so severe.

"Would you stop it already with assuming I'm going to molest you? I have no interest in you. Other than making sure you don't get sick and die on me."

"I don't get sick." She truly didn't. Shifters had an amazing ability to heal from things.

"You might not get sick from normal things, but you spent quite a bit of time, from the looks of you, in the bayou. There are things out there that will make even the toughest of us ill. Swamp fever isn't something to scoff at."

"I don't have a fever. I'm cold." So cold, right down to the marrow of her thin bones.

"Give me a second and we'll work on that." He dropped her onto a bed with a mattress so hard she didn't make a dent.

"I need a blanket." Forget the phone. Right now, she just wanted to get this numbness out of her limbs.

He yanked a cover over her, a thick one. Still, she trembled.

"I'm cold," she complained in a plaintive voice she didn't recognize.

"I should call a doctor."

At the mention, her eyes opened wide and she uttered a frantic, "No. Don't call anyone. No one can know I'm here."

"What's going on, Aria? Who are you running from?"

"The monsters." She giggled.

"What monsters? What are you talking about?"

"Can't say. It's a secret. Shhh." She muttered the words as her eyes closed. "So cold." The shivering wouldn't stop to the point her bones ached.

A heavy sigh filled the silence before the mattress beside her dipped.

In a flash, she popped open her eyes and regarded Constantine, who lay facing her.

"What are you doing?"

"Warming you up. Roll over."

"But—"

"Must you constantly argue? Roll over so I can warm you and leave."

The tough side she'd cultivated as a veneer against the world wanted to protest his help, even if she needed it. She ignored that voice and obeyed

Constantine's deep, rumbled command instead. She tilted onto her side facing away from him.

An arm came around her and yanked her close, tucking her against the massive length of him. The intimacy of the position had her sucking in a breath. Tucked so tightly against him, she could feel the hardness of his frame, but even better, the heat.

He radiated delicious warmth. A soft sigh exhaled from her as her shivering body soaked it in.

A large hand splayed across her belly, spreading warmth of a different kind through her. Her bottom wiggled, inching closer to him. As she felt a certain distinctive hardness, she froze.

"Um, what happened to my not being your type?" she asked as the evidence of a massive erection pressed against her backside.

"You're still not my type, but I am a normal man and you are a woman. Not much I can do to change that. But don't worry. I'm not planning to do anything about it. I am tired, so if you don't mind, can you stop arguing for one minute and go to sleep?"

Not argue? But it was what she did best.

Except, in this instance, she didn't really want to talk him into moving away. In that moment, Aria enjoyed a warmth and peace—*I feel safe*—she'd never enjoyed.

Exhausted from her escape, and safe within the cocoon of his body, Aria fell into a restless slumber.

Chapter Four

No sleep for me tonight.

Constantine, despite his claims to the contrary, found himself much too attracted to Aria to feasibly manage any kind of sleep.

It made no sense. He'd not lied when he told Aria he preferred bigger girls. Taller girls. Women who could handle a man his size.

Aria didn't have an extra ounce of fat on her anywhere. Then again, since she belonged to the avian family of shifters, staying slim wasn't just a necessity, but a fact of life. In order to have the ability to actually fly, bird species needed to remain light.

Everything about her was slim, even her little butt. Little but not unnoticed where it pressed against his groin.

Hisssss.

Talk about pure torture. Never before had an erection of this magnitude plagued him, and without her doing a thing.

What kind of perv lusted after a woman when she was so evidently exhausted and chilled from her ordeal? Sure, he'd climbed into bed with altruistic intentions, but altruism didn't stop the dirty thoughts in his head.

Wrap around her. Squeeze her.

His reptile really didn't see the problem. The man, however, didn't let his baser self dictate his actions.

As warmth returned to her limbs, her body relaxed.

He heard more than saw as Princess hopped onto the bed, a bed with a lower frame so she could make the leap. He opened his eyes and noted his dog's big eyes fixated on Aria's face. Princess let out a small *grr* and *yip*.

"Shh," he hushed. "She's sleeping. Don't wake her."

His tiny dog didn't seem to care. She growled again. Someone didn't like her spot being usurped in his bed.

How cute. His little puppy was jealous. "Come here, baby. Come snuggle with Daddy."

Since he'd gotten Princess a few years ago, rescued actually from a pet store that caught fire, lots of folks eyed their pairing with incredulity. But that was because they just didn't understand. From the moment those huge eyes caught his where she stood in her cage, barking with the ferociousness of a rabid pit bull but the size of a hamster, he'd fallen in love.

His friends mocked his choice in pet only once, unless they had a good dental plan. Some guys loved their cars. Others collected shit. Constantine doted on his dog.

He also pretty much lived by the motto on one of his T-shirts that said, "If my Chihuahua doesn't like you, then neither will I."

As Princess crawled under the blankets and

snuggled up against his spine, he couldn't help but wonder if he might have to revise that stance, though, because, while Princess might not like Aria, he quite did.

Attraction, though, didn't mean he ignored the weirdness about her re-appearance. What did she run from? Where had she spent those missing days?

He and his friends had combed the town, yet no one had seen any trace of Aria after her last visit to Bitten Pint, the local bar.

They did eventually find her things in Bedbug Bites, a bed and breakfast thought closed down. Within that B&B they'd discovered not only her abandoned personal items, but also the body of the owner. More importantly, they'd found some old smuggler tunnels under the house.

However, forget any clues or directions to Aria or the culprits terrorizing their town.

A crooked sheriff set fire to the place and left them back at square one.

But they might now finally have an advantage. *I found Aria.* Actually, she'd found him, but either way, he'd bet a lot of the answers were inside her head. Questions that would have to wait until morning when she woke.

Forget her fatigue. *I should wake her up and demand answers.* While she rested, their town was being stalked. Friends and families fought off attacks, and those who failed went missing.

Who was behind it? Dinoman and dogman, mutant creatures, were at the heart of the conflicts, yet they hadn't come out of nowhere. Someone had created them.

The owner of Bittech, a medical institute that did experiments on shifter blood and genes, claimed innocence and that all their work was sanctioned by the SHC—Shifter High Council, the governing body for their kind.

Should the blame go to Sheriff Pete, whose son, Merrill, appeared involved?

Who could they point the finger at? Who could they punish?

Every trail they followed had led to a dead end. Until now. He couldn't help but inhale the scent of Aria and wonder if, in his arms, slept the missing piece of the puzzle.

What had Aria seen? What did she know? And the bigger question, could he protect her from what she ran from?

Like duh. Of course he would. *I'll crush anyone that lays a hand on her.* And, if they were tasty, eat them.

Chapter Five

The hunters chased her, with raucous calls and murderous intent. Through the woods she sprinted, arms slapping away branches, spitting out the cobwebs that clung to her face as she ran into them.

But she dared not stop or slow down.

They'll kill me if they catch me. Or, worse, they'd do to her what they'd done to countless others. *Make me into a monster.*

She burst free from the foliage and found herself teetering on the edge of a cliff. Arms windmilling, she strove to keep her balance. Down didn't look like an option with its steep incline and sharp rocks. Behind her, a creature bayed, a thing that had once been a man but now was lower than an animal.

I can't go back that way. That left her only one option.

Up.

She flung herself into the air, arms spread, calling forth her eagle. The pain proved excruciating but fleeting. Arms turned into wings. Feet into claws. Her face pulled into a beak while her eyes got razor-sharp vision.

With a mighty pump of her wings, she soared, emitting a laughing caw as the hunters spilled out onto the cliff she'd just perched on, howling their disappointment into the air.

Ha ha. Miss me, miss me. Now you get to—

The heavy weight slammed into her, shocking the breath from her lungs, and she went plummeting down, down, down, in a deadly spiral. The ground rose to meet her and—

"Wake up."

The shaking of her body and barked words had her eyes springing open. For a moment, disorientation assailed her as she cast her gaze frantically about. "Who are you? Where am I?"

"It's okay, Aria. You're safe. It's me, Constantine, remember me? I helped you after you crawled out of the swamp."

Ah yes, the big snake man with the little dog. She recalled him, just like she recalled she'd yet to put a call in to let anyone know where she was.

She struggled to sit up, but didn't make it all the way before dizziness had her clamping her eyes shut and slumping back down.

"What's wrong with me? Why is it so hot in here?" She managed to thrash her legs and push off the covers.

A chilly hand pressed against her forehead. "You're burning up."

Burning with desire. Through slitted eyes, she regarded Constantine. The man proved quite attractive in daylight. "You're cute."

His brows rose. "Excuse me?"

"And polite. Do you have a girlfriend?" She squirmed on the bed as fire coursed through her veins.

"I really don't see that it's any of your business."

Aria's lips curved as she stretched out. "I hope you don't because she wouldn't like it if she knew I was sleeping in your bed."

"I don't have a girlfriend, so you needn't worry."

"Me, worry?" She giggled, a bubbly sound that went with the floating sensation inside her head. "I'd kick her ass. I don't share."

"I think you're delirious."

"I think you're right," she mumbled. It didn't take his remark for her to realize her thinking seemed off.

"We really should call a doctor."

"No doctor. No one can know where I am. Not even Thea." She flailed her hands and gripped his loose T-shirt. "Promise me you won't tell. Promise."

He blew out a breath. "This is crazy. You need a doctor. You've got the swamp fever."

"So give me some pills. Just swear you won't tell anyone I'm here. You'll be in danger. Everyone is in danger."

"I've got some antibiotics from when I cut myself on the job. I didn't need them, but the emergency room doctor was a normal dude and didn't know that. I'll go grab them. Don't go anywhere. Princess, guard her."

As if Aria could go anywhere. Her limbs felt weighted, concrete filling her bones.

Something blew hotly in her face, and she opened eyes she didn't realize had shut to see a tiny furry face glaring at her.

"What do you want?" she muttered.

Grrr.

"Don't worry, squeaky toy, the feeling is mutual."

And she was obviously more delusional than she realized, seeing as how she conversed with a dog, if something that wouldn't even make a meal could be called a dog.

Something wet and chilly slopped onto her forehead. "Open your mouth." Fingers probed at her lips, and she spread them enough for him to slide some pills into her mouth. The bitter taste had her grimacing and complaining.

"Oh, gross."

"Drink." The stern command came as he lifted her upper body and pressed the rim of a glass against her lips.

She swallowed. She didn't have a choice. It was that or drown.

"You're mean," she muttered.

"Says the girl I've done nothing but help so far."

"I need a phone." While her body seemed determined to melt into a puddle of useless goo, her mind got moments of clarity.

To her surprise, he pulled a cell phone from his pocket. She grabbed it with shaking hands that dropped it.

"Fuck."

"Not now, you're kind of sick," Constantine retorted.

"You are not funny. But you're still cute." Ugh. Someone shoot her. It seemed she couldn't trust her mouth to keep her inner thoughts secret.

"So cute I'll help you dial. What's the number?"

Number? Dammit. She didn't remember her boss's number by heart. It was programmed in her phone, and she no longer had that sucker. Which again sucked because it was only a few months old. It would cost her a fortune to buy out her stupid contract.

Fingers snapped in front of her. "Earth to Aria, come in, Aria."

She turned her gaze back to him, trying to focus but having a hard time. "Would you stop moving?" she complained.

"I'm not. You're sick and need to lie down."

"Not until I call Thea. I need to know she's safe. I worried her the last time I called, and I shouldn't have done that. But I had to. Just in case I didn't come back."

"You are back now. You're safe."

"Safe?" Again, the hysterical laughter burst free. "No one is safe. I have to stay away from her. I should stay away from you, too." She swung her legs over the edge of the bed, only to have them immediately moved back onto the mattress.

"You're not going anywhere."

"You don't understand, they're looking for me."

"Who is?"

"The monsters." She slapped a hand over her mouth. She shouldn't have told him about that.

"I know about the monsters, Aria."

"You do?"

He nodded. "I've been looking for them for a while now, but have not had any luck. Do you know where they are?"

"Yes." They were in cages. A whole row of them.

"Where, Aria?"

She opened her mouth, but instead of spewing words, she spewed water.

In other circumstances, she might have been appalled that she'd tossed the meager contents of her tummy on the man trying to help her, but given her limbs chose that moment to go spastic, she concentrated more on not biting her tongue off.

But uncontrollable spasms didn't mean she didn't utter a very apt, "Fuck!"

Chapter Six

Another man might have taken offense to the fact that the woman he loaned his bed to barfed on his favorite T-shirt—"I <3 Chihuahuas." However, Constantine wasn't a dick.

As Aria's eyes rolled back in her head and her body convulsed, he acted. He yanked his television remote from the nightstand and wedged it between her teeth. Then he straddled her waist, pinning her body with his own, his hands clamped around her wrists, holding them over her head lest she shake herself right off the bed.

It was at that moment his mother chose to walk in.

"Constantine Xavier Boudreaux. What on earth are you doing to that poor girl?" she yelled.

Uh-oh, she'd used all his names. "Can't you see I'm helping her? She's having a seizure." And a good one, too. It vibrated her whole body.

"I'll call the doctor."

But that is the one thing Aria doesn't want.

Before his mother could pivot and do exactly that, he barked, "Don't. You can't call anyone."

"Are you insane? The woman is obviously sick."

Yes, but if it was the swamp fever, it would pass if he treated it with the pills he had. *But what if it's something else?*

He wasn't a trained medical professional. He couldn't care for her. Yet, he remembered the terror in her eyes, the plea to not let anyone know she was here.

I promised.

The tremors eased. Aria's body went limp, and while she remained pale, her breathing whooshed in and out in an even cadence.

He climbed off her. "It stopped."

"I see that," was his mother's sarcastic reply. "But those spasms could come back."

"If they do, or she gets worse, then I'll call the doc. In the meantime, she asked me to keep her presence quiet."

"Why? What did she do? Is she a criminal? Who is she?"

"This is Aria."

His mother's brows arched. "Isn't that the girl you've been looking for?"

"Yes. I found her by the swamp last night, exhausted and running from someone." Or something.

"Do your friends know you've found her?"

He shook his head, and his mother frowned.

"Don't give me that look. I'm going to let them know, but I thought I'd wait until she could tell them herself." Not a complete cop-out. They'd already know if Aria hadn't gone into convulsions.

"I don't like this." His mother's lips pursed. "There is something rotten in this town."

"There is. But don't worry, Mom, we're going

to find it." And crush it.

If only he could crush whatever ailed Aria. He called in ill to work so he could spend the day tending her. Not that there was much to tend. She laid there, still as a corpse, her skin sporting a waxy pallor. The shallow breaths she took seemed barely enough to keep her heart pumping.

As he kept a vigil by her bedside, Princess on his lap helping, he surfed the Web on his phone, searching for symptoms of swamp fever and how to treat it. Except he wasn't sure that she suffered from it.

Sure, she presented many of the symptoms with the fever, the chills, and the vomiting. However, those convulsions weren't typical. They also didn't return. The fever did, though, and he spent that night sponging her on and off with a cold washcloth, battling the extreme heat radiating from her skin.

When it spiked at a hundred and seven, just past dawn the next day, he was ready to call the doctor, except, as he started to dial, Aria came to life.

She sucked in a huge breath. Her eyes opened wide. She sat bolt upright in bed.

He put down his phone and approached her slowly, noting her pupils seemed to track him, just like her nostrils flared as if testing his scent.

While subtle, he noted the fine hairs on her arm rise, and her gaze narrowed. She bore the look of an animal debating fight or flight.

"Where am I?"

"In my bed."

"Where is that? And who are you?" she asked, a hint of impatience in her tone.

A furrow marred his brow as he replied. "We're in my house on the outskirts of Bitten Point. As for who I am, don't you remember me finding you in the swamp?"

"No." Flatly stated. "I don't remember coming to this town. Or you. Or me for that matter." The lines in her forehead deepened, and she whispered her next words. "Who am I?"

Chapter Seven

The panic in her threatened to overwhelm. Everywhere she looked, she drew a blank. She didn't recognize a single thing. Not the room with the paneled walls painted a medium gray. Not the scarred wooden dresser with the small stereo on top. She especially didn't remember the big guy towering at the foot of the bed, watching her intently.

Is he my boyfriend?

He was certainly attractive enough with a rugged face complemented by a square jawline, piercing eyes, and a strong nose. The size of him proved impressive. How did he manage to find shirts that wide?

And who the hell wore a shirt that said, "Don't get between a man and his Chihuahua"? She couldn't help an incredulous note as she read it aloud.

A furry rat chose that moment to hop onto the bed and bare its teeth.

Without even pausing to think about it, she leaned forward and growled back. "Don't start that shit with me, Princess."

"You remember the dog's name but not mine?"

How offended he sounded. She shrugged. "Can't remember mine either. Guess we're even."

"You're Aria."

Her nose wrinkled. "That's an awfully girly name."

"Maybe on account you're a girl."

For some reason, that made her snort. "Okay. Whatever. What's your name then?"

"Constantine."

"That name seems familiar. Wasn't he an angel of some kind?"

"I'm hardly angelic."

So he claimed, yet she couldn't help but have the feeling he could easily assume the role of protector.

He keeps me safe.

An odd assertion to have, yet it felt right.

"Are you my boyfriend?" That would explain why she was in his bed wearing a T-shirt and nothing else, a T-shirt that she doubted belonged to her and not just on account of the stupid dog saying on the front. The massive tent of fabric hung on her slim frame.

"No, we are not dating."

Was it her, or did she sense a "yet" in the air? "If we're not dating, then why am I in your bed, wearing your shirt and nothing else?" Not even panties, she suddenly noted. "You fucking pervert. Did you drug me? Is that why I can't remember anything?" Her eyes widened as she accused loudly.

"What? No. Hell no. I wouldn't do such a thing."

"Says you."

"Yeah, says me, and I don't appreciate the

fucking accusation, especially seeing as how I took you into my home after finding you half dead in the swamp, gave you my bed, and just spent the last twenty-four hours mopping your sweaty ass and forcing you to guzzle fluids, which, I might add, you barfed on me, trying to keep you from dying."

"If you're so concerned, why didn't you call a doctor?"

He gaped at her. "Why? Because you bloody well begged me not to."

"And you listened to me?"

"I'm wishing I hadn't, believe me, lady."

"I'm no lady." The words came out of her with familiarity, as if she'd said them many a time before.

"You're also not a gracious guest. Gonna claim you forgot your manners with your name?"

"No. I think that part of my delightful personality is all me," she replied with a smirk.

He laughed. "You're definitely very forthright. And I guess you deserve a pass given the situation. But let's get one thing clear. I am only trying to help you. So work with me."

Work with him or just plain work him? Playing with that bod would require some serious climbing skills. But now wasn't the time or place. "Now that we've kind of ascertained you're not a murdering rapist," or so she hoped, "can you tell me a bit more about who I am and how I got here?"

So he did. He told her of some girl called Cynthia who had come looking for Aria when she went missing. How they searched the town for her to no avail. Told her of the attacks by impossible creatures. The missing people. The dead ones, too. And, finally, her arrival the previous night.

When he was done, she whistled. "Damn, angel. That's some crazy story."

"Angel?"

Her lips curved. "From the sounds of it, you played the part of my guardian angel. Saving me from the monsters in the swamp and then watching over me as I fought off whatever bug I caught out there."

"Just doing the right thing. Us shifters have to stick together."

"Shifters?" She wrinkled her nose. "What the heck is that supposed to mean?"

He regarded her with a flat stare. "Shifter? You know, as in you turn into an eagle. I turn into a snake. While we're different species, we still are basically the same kind."

"Hold on there, angel. I listened to your messed up fantasy story of monsters coming after folks because you're cute. But if you think I'm going to believe for one second that you're a..." Her voice trailed off as the man before her rippled. As in his skin undulated and changed, turning from tanned, smooth flesh into something darker, mottled, scaly.

"Fuck!" She screamed the word even as she leaped from the bed. Her feet hit the floor, but her legs wobbled and refused to hold her. Down she went, knees hitting hard, yet that didn't stop her from crawling for the door, scrabbling before that *thing* came after her.

"Sssstop it."

"Or what?"

"Or I'll sssssic my dog on you," was the monster's sibilant reply.

As if summoned, the little dog from hell flew past Aria and braced herself in the doorway. A lip curled back on the muzzle, baring sharp teeth as she uttered a ferocious growl.

Aria pressed her forehead to the floor and muttered, "This isn't fucking happening. I must still be sick. Hallucinating. Out of my freaking mind."

"Or," a deep voice rumbled from behind her, "you could admit that maybe I'm telling the truth."

Given his voice sounded normal again, she canted her head to the side to peek at him. Constantine regarded her with a serious expression. A human expression.

"People aren't supposed to turn into things."

"Humans don't, but we do."

We? Aria might not recall much, not even her own face at the moment, but surely he didn't speak the truth. Wouldn't she know if she was this shifter creature he claimed?

She blinked, and suddenly, the room around her disappeared. She soared, high in a clear blue sky, cold wind rushing past her face.

Another blink and the room returned. But it didn't bring her sanity with it.

Brawny arms wrapped around her upper torso and plucked her from the floor as if she weighed nothing but a feather.

My feathers are lush, and fluffy.

An odd thought to have, yet it felt right. True. But fucked up.

While Constantine might have manhandled her off the floor, he didn't deposit her back in bed. Instead, he headed out of the bedroom into the hall.

"Where are you taking me?"

"You need a shower."

A certain amount of feminine pride raised its head. "Are you saying I stink?"

"Yup."

Perhaps the real her, the one with memories, might have taken offense. This Aria, however, laughed. "Touché. I guess I am pretty rank." The sour smell of sweat permeated not only her skin, but also the shirt she wore.

He set her on her feet in the bathroom, but her legs still wouldn't hold her.

Down she dropped. He moved quicker, slipping to his knees and catching her. For balance, she threw her arms around his neck.

"Nice moves, angel."

"If anyone deserves that name, it's the girl with actual wings."

She snickered. "I might not remember much at the moment, but I'm pretty sure I lost my chance of earning those a long time ago." No way she had wings. Not ever. The idea of her having some eagle inside her that might burst out at any moment? Entirely too crazy. "So if you're not an angel out to save me, then what are you?"

"The snake in the garden, I'm beginning to think." He rose quickly as he muttered the words, setting her upright and propped against the sink.

The comforting strength of his hands left her waist, their loss immediately noted. *I don't want him touching me.* Total lie. She might not feel quite herself at the moment, but she couldn't help but notice Constantine exuded *man.* He moved with a freaky grace and had the most deliciously toned body, if huge. He treated her with kid gloves, yet he dared to challenge with his words—and, yes, even tease her. Tease her senses and skin.

What is wrong with me?

Why did she find herself unable to stop thinking of him? Perhaps if she stopped staring in his direction?

She looked down at her toes—*pink toenails?* Odd, she wouldn't have taken herself as someone who'd choose such a girly color. *Heck, I wouldn't have thought I went for pedicures either.*

But it wasn't her choice.

"You have to get your toes done," Thea said for like the millionth time as she lounged in the ass-pounding massage chair, feet propped in front of her so the attendant could scrub the hell out of them. "I mean, think of it. What if you meet a hunk, and you want to do the naughty tango?"

"First off, it's fucking, not dancing, and second, I still don't get what my toes have to do with this. It's not like I'm going to shove them in his mouth to suck."

Thea grabbed at her perfectly straightened hair—a job that took over two hours of extreme patience. "Toe sucking? Never. That would tickle way too much. I'm talking about having your toes look good for when he's got you flat on your back and your legs are hiked with your feet up around his shoulders. Which reminds me, we're also hitting the wax today, my hairy Sasquatch friend."

A heavy groan left Aria. "Why do you do this to me?"

"Because if you don't look good, I don't look good." Thea grinned as Aria shook her head. *"How about because you need to get laid in a bad way."*

Yeah, she did, but it wasn't her fault most of the men Aria met were tools, as in guys she'd rather slap than fuck. *"Fine. We'll do the legs, but stay away from my girly parts."*

"I agree. Leave that bush hairy. The whole seventies retro thing is totally in. You should see how curly mine has gotten."

Slapping her hands over her ears, Aria screeched. "Too much info."

"…doing?"

"Hunh." Aria snapped out of the vivid mental video. She'd just flashed on a memory. That was a good thing. Perhaps this amnesia thing wasn't permanent.

Snap. Constantine clicked his fingers in front of her a second time. "I am wondering if you should go back to bed."

With a little difficulty, she focused her gaze on him. Before she realized it, her fingers brushed the skin of his cheek, a cheek that looked utterly normal right now.

Stillness invaded him, and she could have sworn he even held his breath. She could understand that reaction because she held her breath, too. The moment between them stretched, almost visible, a thing of awareness, curiosity, intimacy. She let him into her space.

Am I usually closed off?

Usually, yes, but now…now she wanted to touch. So she did. The fingers on his cheek pressed against warm flesh. Not monster. Not snake. Soft, supple skin met her feathery exploration of his face.

Her hand moved down, the tips of her digits encountering some bristly roughness.

"You have a five o'clock shadow."

"Yes. Why wouldn't I?"

Her gaze rose to meet his. "You're a snake. I would have imagined you as hairless."

Big fingers clasped hers and drew her hand to the top of his head. The soft hair threaded like silk through her raking fingers. "Does this feel fake to you?"

"It's so fine in texture."

"Yeah, and to give you credit, you're probably not far off the mark when you mention the hairless thing. My chest is pretty bare. But the good news is, so is my back."

She made a moue. "Too much info, angel."

"No, too much info is saying I've got a full bush down there."

No peek down needed when her cheeks brightened at the obviousness of his claim. But his bold words did draw a feisty retort. "Is this your way of saying you've got a snake in the grass?"

Laughter barked from him, loud and genuine. "That was fucking funny. But more seriously, we snakes get a bad rep. Just because people are scared of us doesn't make us inherently bad. I'd like to think I'm a decent guy who just happens to have been born with a cool ability."

"So you are born? Not bitten or…"

"Or what? Did I drink blood? Can I walk in daylight? Is it true my tongue can make you scream?"

"Conceited much?"

He winked. "Not conceit if it's true." He turned away from her and went to the doorway. "I will leave the door open so I can hear you in case you run into trouble."

"You're not going to stay and watch?" She couldn't help but tease.

For a second, she could have sworn his eyes changed just a little. A low, almost yellow glow entered them, the pupils narrowed and slitted.

How dangerous he looked in that moment. Inhuman. She shivered, yet it was not in fear.

Mine.

What a strange idea, and certainly not why she held out her hand and said, "Can you help me get into the shower?"

Okay, she might not know herself too well yet, but she would wager good money that she wasn't the type to ask for help, from anyone. Especially not some guy. A hot guy.

Oh my God, I think I might be a slut.

Well, that would suck, yet explain why, despite her current mental dilemma, she still found herself hugely attracted to him, attracted and totally flirting with him.

Good thing he knew how to resist.

"I think you'll be fine. I'll leave you alone now. Holler when you're done." He fled from the washroom.

Asshole, she thought with a glare in that direction.

Coward. He had disappeared awfully quick. Unless… Clarity widened her eyes. No normal, single guy would turn down a chance to help a woman get naked and into a shower.

"Holy shit, he's gay," she muttered aloud.

"Am not." Constantine suddenly framed the door.

"How the hell did you hear that? I thought you left."

"I told you I wouldn't go far."

Not far. He must have stood just outside the door. She didn't know if she should call him a perv or preen that he couldn't bring himself to go farther.

"So you like girls then?"

"Yes."

She cocked her head. "What about me?"

Did he look as taken aback as she felt? There was being forthright, and then there was balls out on the table, directly asking.

Shit. *What is wrong with me?*

Blink and the scenery changed. She was in a cell now, a cell whose walls she'd memorized.

"What is wrong with me?" she asked again, not that anyone bothered to answer.

A glance to her side had her gasping.

The needle moved toward her arm steadily, the glass vial attached to it full of an amber liquid with hints of darkness.

Don't touch me with that. *Yet she couldn't move, not a single limb, pull as she might. The straps on the gurney held her tight.*

They'd tied her down like an animal because they were treating her like an animal. No better than a lab rat.

"*This will only hurt a little bit,*" *the man said. He bore a fringe of white around his crown, and his facial skin held the creases of time. He wore the long white coat of a doctor yet didn't wear a stethoscope around his neck, nor did she like his bedside manner. After all, what kind of doctor tied down their patient?*

A mad-scientist type.

"*Don't touch me,*" *she growled.* "*Don't you dare.*"

Another face came into view, sporting a smirk wide as a barn door and begging for a smack. "*This is what happens to little girls who come snooping.*"

"*What are you afraid of me finding?*" *she challenged.*

"*Nothing now. You'll have more important things to worry about in a minute than whether or not our operation is on the up and up. Staying alive being the first and foremost.*"

"*You can't do this,*" *she repeated, eyes frozen to the slow descent of the needle. She thrashed as hard as she could, her slight frame twisting, yet not even coming close to loosening her bonds.*

No escape. They've grounded me. I'm caged. *Her breathing came fast and furious while her heart pounded.*

"*No,*" *she screamed as the sharp tip of the needle pierced her skin.*

No one listened.

The plunger depressed, and liquid fire entered her veins.

Chapter Eight

Standing in the doorway, a voyeuristic perv, Constantine knew he should go. *I need to go.* And farther than two feet from the door this time so Aria could shower. He truly meant to leave her alone, except her eyes glazed over and he knew her mind went wandering again, leaving nobody home to pilot the body.

Already in motion, he caught the way her body tensed then relaxed all at once, letting gravity yank at her.

Once again, Aria fell, and once again, he caught her, but only because he slid under her baseball style so she landed in his arms and lap.

He prevented her from getting hurt yet… *She wouldn't be fainting in the bathroom, though, if I hadn't pushed for her to shower.* What she really needed more than a bath was more rest and some food.

"That's it, little birdie, back to bed you go."

"Little birdie as a name is utterly offensive," she snapped with a touch of heat.

"Says the lady calling me angel."

"Would you prefer I call you little birdie?" And, yes, the brat did aim her gaze downward.

"Ain't nothing little about me, *chickadee.*"

Her gaze narrowed. "Are you seriously trying to antagonize me?"

"I would never do that, *starling*." He did have to bite the inside of his cheek at that one.

Exasperation blew between her lips. "Stop it."

"Or what?" he challenged.

A sly look entered her gaze. "I see what you're doing. If you want to kiss me, just get it over with," she dared back. "I know you want to."

Damn her, he did. "I don't," he lied.

"Why am I so utterly certain you're lying about that?" she mused aloud.

"Your animal instinct is guiding you, even if you don't recognize it."

"It should guide me to some water and soap. I reek."

"No water. Bed."

"I am totally taking a shower," she stubbornly insisted as she pushed at his chest and struggled to get off his lap.

"Like hell. You just about face-planted again."

"At least this time there's no poop."

"You remember meeting me?"

She grinned. "I guess I do. So see, I'm fine. Getting stronger every minute. I got faint because I remembered something."

"Are you sure it's a memory?"

"Pretty sure, that or I have a sick imagination." As she told him what she recalled, his eyes widened.

"They injected you with something. Now we really need to get you to a doctor."

Short hair flew and whipped her cheeks as she shook her head. "No." She pushed hard enough to get to her feet. "We can't tell anyone."

"We have to tell someone," he argued. "Cynthia and my friends are still looking for you."

"Fine. We'll call her and let her know I'm alive and to stop looking. But we're calling after my shower."

She did seem much steadier. Also, he knew the reviving effect of a shower after a strenuous night. Firemen often came home exhausted, dirty, and needing a moment to clear their mind and wash the world from their skin.

"As my *dove* commands." Rising also to his feet, Constantine leaned over and peeled the vinyl shower curtain back, revealing the smooth, seamless plastic shield he'd installed during a long weekend after he tore out the cracked and stained tile.

"I am going to peck your eyes out," she grumbled as she brushed past him, lifting a foot to step into the tub.

"I've got something better you can pet."

Constantine didn't usually resort to bawdy flirting. Where these dirty innuendos came from he couldn't have said. Probably Daryl's bad influence. Yet, he'd known Daryl for years and never used them before, so why now? Why her?

Most women would have retorted with shock at his bold words. Rejection was possible, too.

What he didn't expect was Aria, with a mischievous glint in her eyes, to pop a pearly-toothed grin. "You're the man with all the bold words. Well, let's see how you stack up when under pressure." Aria stepped fully into the shower and lifted her arms. "Take the shirt off. I dare you."

She didn't just do that.

She had.

I dare you. Those three words were the downfall of many a man. Constantine would like to say he held the strength to resist. He didn't. See, he believed in the man club, the one with a double-standard, fucked-up sense of rules. The membership card might only exist in the minds and thoughts of men, but that didn't make it any less real or potent. And he knew his damned card would get shredded for sure if he didn't strip the shirt off the sexy woman in the shower.

I must do this for the sake of mankind.

Gulp.

Be strong.

While his T-shirt hung loose on Aria's frame, it didn't dangle much past her hips. He could practically see the vee at the top of her thighs.

I never did see if she trims or not.

Personally, he liked a girl who went natural. Something to nuzzle.

Water from the shower began to spray the white cotton she wore, making it cling, especially around her chest.

How could he have thought before her breasts were too small? Never. He gladly admitted his mistake. They were perfect. Two perfect round domes with protruding peaks begging for his mouth.

"Are you going to do it, *angel?*" Her words

teased huskily over his skin.

Do. Her.

No, wait. She meant something else. The shirt. The shirt had to come off.

On stiff legs, he clambered into the shower, placing himself across from her. Given the tight fit, it put him close to her.

She peeked at him. "Not leaving yourself much room to take the shirt off, big guy."

He leaned down until his mouth hovered just over hers. "I need to be close to do this."

Rip.

Chapter Nine

Okay, this might really make her a whore, but holy fucking hot. When Constantine gripped that shirt and tore it in two as the last of his words brushed her lips with hot air, it was like seriously off the charts, sexy, hot.

"Challenge met," he murmured, brushing his mouth ever so lightly over hers. "Now shower, my smelly duck."

Before she could screech at him, he fled, leaving only his soft chuckle floating behind.

He also left behind one really aroused woman, one who wanted to chase him down for vengeance, the naked kind, but also a woman who found herself laughing at his deviousness. "A point for the snake."

And a thank-you. Things got pretty intense between them for a moment. Events might have gone from "help me" to "fuck me" with just a single kiss. Even if she'd been a slut in her previous life, it didn't mean she had to be one now. Time to get her head out of her pussy and back onto what happened around her.

As she stood under the spray, its reviving heat stimulating every part of her body, she reviewed a few key facts from what Constantine explained to her.

One. *I am in danger.* In and running from it by the sounds of it.

Two. Someone had done something to her. Injected her with a foreign drug. As such, she couldn't necessarily rely on her instincts or even her rationality. Did the fluid they inject her with cause any kind of mental impairment or an as-yet-unknown physical one?

As she lifted her face into the hot water, she wondered if her amnesia was related to the injection.

It didn't take long to clean herself. She didn't want to waste time. Now that she seemed recovered, at least bodily wise, she had to find some answers.

Such as, what do I look like?

So far in her visions, she'd seen other people. Oddly enough, while she had a sense of self, she had no visual image to go with it.

Stepping from the shower, she grabbed a towel and wrapped it around her moist body. She tucked the corner between her small breasts, cinching it.

Over the vanity, she spotted a mirror. She stood before it, hands braced on the vinyl top that held a pink, seashell-shaped ceramic sink. Very retro.

I'm stalling.

The steam from the shower clouded the mirror, and she leaned forward to wipe at it with her hand. It didn't take long to clear a swath and see herself.

This is *me.* While she didn't recall seeing her image before, it still seemed familiar. Aria stood pretty short, which she already knew. She noted other facts, such as the fine bone structure, the pointed chin. The finely arched brows. The long, sloping nose. The thin lips with the slightest indent on the top. Her hair, shoulder length and bobbed. With a…

"Aaaaah!"

Her shrill scream brought Constantine running. He skidded into the bathroom. "What is it? What's wrong?"

"My hair," she gasped.

"What about it?" he replied. "It's clean. Wet, though, but there's a dryer under the sink if you need one. No big emergency."

"Not that, you idiot," she grumbled. "Look at this." She yanked a hank of it in the air for him to inspect.

"Yeah?" He blinked at her.

She explained slowly, as if to a moron. It was that or smack him. "It's white."

"Yeah."

"Don't you get it?" she exclaimed.

"No."

Such a man. They never noticed what was right in front of them. "It's not supposed to be white."

"How do you know that? Did you remember something else?"

"No, but that doesn't mean I don't remember that *this* isn't supposed to be white." She shook the offensive chunk.

"Are you sure about that? Because you had it when I first met you."

His reply took her aback. "What do you mean it was already there?"

"I didn't see it when you first crawled out of the muck on account you were so dirty."

She scowled at his reminder.

"But after you rinsed, I saw it. And you've had it ever since. Although"—he reached out a hand to touch the white band—"it does seem wider than before."

"This is great. Just great. First I'm apparently being chased by something in the swamp after being missing for a while. Then I find out I've been injected with some weird sort of mutant virus."

"We don't know that for sure."

She glared at him for his interruption. "Oh please, you don't believe that for a minute. And now, look at this, white hair. It's wrong, I tell you. So wrong. I'm only twenty-four."

"You remembered your age?"

She blinked as he took her completely off topic. "I did. Damn. That's weird how stuff keeps filtering its way back in."

"And you'll remember more, I'm sure, once you eat."

"Food?" At the mere query, her stomach rumbled. "Yes, food. I could totally go for some fried calamari right now."

"Seafood? Did I say you were an eagle? More like a seagull. Get dressed and we'll go get some."

She shook her head. "Impossible. I don't dare go out until I remember more. And, besides, you said I had to call Thea."

"Calling Cynthia will only take a few minutes. Then we can pop out."

"I have no clothes."

"Actually, I found some of Renny's stuff in the dryer. My mom has this habit of stealing hers and Caleb's and my nephew's laundry and doing it."

"That's a weird habit."

"She's got a laundry fetish. It's harmless. Now stop stalling."

At his gentle tug, she followed him from the bathroom back to his bedroom, where Princess lay on his bed, glaring at Aria.

"I left you a pile of clothes..." He trailed off. "That's odd. I could have sworn I left them on the bed."

"Are you talking about those?" Aria pointed to a puddle of fabric on the floor.

"Princess. Did you drag those clothes onto the floor?" He gave her a stern voice, one meant to chastise.

His dog rolled onto her back, four paws in the air, and gave him puppy eyes.

It was stupidly cute. So cute. Aria steeled herself against it. However, Constantine melted like a marshmallow over a hot flame. "Who needs a belly rub? Does Daddy's sweet girl need one?"

Aria sighed before she muttered, "That is seriously pathetic."

"I think someone is jealous you're getting a belly rub, Princess," the jerk smugly retorted, fingers tickling someone other than Aria.

Oh hell no. He's mine. He's...

The jealousy came on fast and furious. She needed to counter it. Needed him to go away—and stop scratching that damned dog.

"I am not asking you for a belly rub." She whipped the towel off and flung it to the floor. "But I do have a magic button that likes getting stroked." She arched a brow at him, and she could have laughed when he fled the room with a shouted, "You play dirty."

I might, but damn, it's fun. It would be even more fun if he stayed instead of running.

Quickly, she dressed, the clothes he'd found loose on her, but at least they covered all the important bits.

With a tentative tread, she exited the bedroom and made her way down the hall. Just out of her sight, she could hear a cupboard slamming shut along with a drawer.

The home didn't have an open floor plan, so she went from a hall right into a simple kitchen and found Constantine. He had his back partially turned from her as he poured them hot water from a kettle into mugs.

"I don't drink tea." She preferred coffee. Black. And strong enough to make her feathers protrude like quills. Another fact about herself.

"Me either. I'm not big on caffeine, but chocolate, on the other hand"—he handed her a mug—"is the beverage of champions."

Hot cocoa? She raised the cup to her lips and breathed deep of the rich cocoa scent. "Nice." Actually heavenly. She plopped onto a stool, closed her eyes, and inhaled again, triggering another mental movie.

Her finger crooked around the handle of the fine china cup. A peek over its rim showed it held hot cocoa, with little marshmallows bobbing on the surface. Steam rose and tickled her nose with the rich chocolate smell.

Aria raised it to her lips and took a sip, just a tiny one so she didn't burn her tongue. Her taste buds exploded with pleasure at the perfect mix. Sweet, with a hint of bitter to showcase it.

Very yummy and how nice of the lady who ran the bed and breakfast to make it for her. Even better, the owner of the B&B had delivered it to her door.

Talk about excellent service.

"Pancakes and bacon sound all right, dearie?" the owner of the B&B asked as she set a domed plate on a small table by the window that had a pair of facing chairs.

"Sounds awesome." Aria took another sip of the hot cocoa then a long pull of the liquid. A hearty breakfast sounded like just the thing she needed before she went out and began her research on the town and, more specifically, Bittech. She'd arrived only the day before and had spent the afternoon and evening familiarizing herself with town and the local bar.

Seating herself at the chair, she grinned as the landlady whipped off the cover of the dome and revealed a plate stacked with fluffy pancakes and crisp bacon. She set her cup down, and it was promptly refilled.

"Thank you." Odd how the words came out slowly. Actually, she felt kind of sluggish, maybe because the chocolate didn't have the much-needed morning caffeine jolt. But sugar was a good substitute.

Aria chugged the contents of the cup, only to feel her

eyes get heavier, the lids tugging down, trying to shut. The fingers holding the cup relaxed, and it fell, spilling hot cocoa everywhere. The cup wasn't the only thing falling.

The pancakes provided a soft landing for her face.

"They drugged me!" Aria exclaimed as she snapped out of memory lane.

"Who did?" Constantine asked from where he leaned against the counter, both of his big hands wrapped around the super-sized mug.

"The lady at the B&B. What was it called?" She tapped her chin.

"Bedbug Bites," he supplied.

"Yes. That's it. The broad who runs it drugged my cocoa." The nerve. Aria slammed her cup down, sloshing the contents.

He arched a single brow as he took a sip from his mug before saying, "Is this your way of saying you think I'm like her and trying to drug you with cocoa?"

She frowned at him. "Of course not. I trust you." She really did. Odd that. "I'll prove it." She grabbed the mug and chugged the contents before slamming it down again. "Ta da."

"I don't suppose you recall anyone ever telling you that you're crazy as a loon."

"Would you stop with the bird names?"

"No."

"You suck."

"Any time."

She glared. "Not everything is grounds for sexual innuendo."

"That's because you lack man-spective."

"What's that mean? On second thought, I don't want to know." Her tummy rumbled, giving her the out she needed. "What are you making us to eat? I don't suppose you have some bacon?"

"No bacon, but I think we have some leftover chicken wings."

Her nose wrinkled. "Cannibal."

For a moment, a look of horror crossed his face. "I'm sorry—I didn't think—"

She snickered. "I'm kidding. As far as I recall, I eat meat." The innuendo proved too blatant to ignore, so she rolled with it. "I especially love sausage. The long, thick kind." His gaze heated as she leaned forward and whispered, "The longer the better, so I can bite the tip off. Crunch."

He winced. "I guess I deserved that."

A giggle bubbled out of her. "Not entirely your fault. I think we're both to blame for setting the other off. Before we totally make this awkward, where's the phone so I can call Thea?"

"Use my cell." He slid it to her across the counter. She snagged it and dialed. Then paused.

"What's wrong?" he asked.

"How do I know this is the right number?"

"You don't, so hit the call button and find out who's on the other end."

True. The worst that could happen was she dialed a wrong number. The phone rang and rang until a guy answered it.

"Hey, Constantine. What are you doing calling Cyn's phone?"

For a moment, Aria froze at the unfamiliar

voice. "Who is this? Where's Thea?" Concern over a girl she barely remembered made her tense.

"This is Daryl, her boyfriend, and I am still trying to figure out—Cyn, hand that back." The phone made a few noises as it got manhandled, but eventually, the static quieted and a perky voice said, "Cynthia here. Who am I speaking to?"

"Thea?"

"Aria! Is that really you?"

"Yes it's me." At least in body. The mind they still had to work on.

"Where have you been? I've been worried sick about you."

"I've been around. Dealing with stuff." Like a giant dude and his vicious dog.

As if sensing her stray thought, Princess barked at her, right by her ankle. Were there any arteries down there she needed to worry about? Just in case, Aria tucked her feet behind the rung on the stool.

"Where are you? I want to see you. Are you with Constantine? Is that why you're calling from his phone?"

"Yes. No. Kind of. But you can't tell anyone. I mean it, Thea. Not a soul can know. I think I'm in trouble." Talking to this woman proved easy, familiar even.

"I think everyone in town is in trouble," Thea said quietly.

"You should leave."

"So everyone keeps telling me. Actually, Daryl is the biggest pain in the ass about it, but I'm not going anywhere. Where Daryl stays, I stay."

"I told you we should have stayed in bed," was his less-than-subtle shout from the background.

"I told you my mom was getting the new one delivered today."

Thea's mom was here? Aria could see her in her mind's eye, buxom and with even wilder hair than Thea, holding out a tray of fresh-baked sesame seed cookies.

Perhaps Constantine was right. Maybe seeing and talking to people would keep jogging the memories.

"Your mom is in Bitten Point?"

"Dad, too."

"Why? What's going on? And since when do you have a boyfriend?" Because, as far as she could recall, Cynthia was single. Or so Aria thought. Kind of hard to tell with the memory thing.

"I do now, and we've kind of shacked up together. It's kind of serious."

Just how many days had Aria lost? "How long has it been?"

"Not long, I know. Totally crazy, but I can't help myself, Aria. I met Daryl, and it was like *boom*."

"More like snore," he interrupted again. "Or aren't you going to explain you drugged me so you could molest me at your leisure?"

"I did not molest you. Much." Giggle. "Sorry, Aria. You don't need to hear that stuff. Because I'm hoping you're doing that stuff with a certain guy we both know. Hint. Hint."

"It's not like that," she hastened to explain.

"He's just helping me out." Helping her out of clothes, but then doing nothing about the fire he started. *He's not a very good fireman, obviously.*

"I'm sure he's helping you. Helping you so much that you don't have time to put on some clothes and visit with a friend."

"I'll have you know I am fully dressed."

"For how long?" Thea snickered.

Good question, given just glancing at him made certain parts of her heat. "Anyhow, the reason I called was to say don't look for me. I'm fine."

"Fine and yet you're acting awful weird and secretive."

"I have my reasons. Please, Thea. Trust me on this."

A big sigh came through on the line. "I guess if you're with Constantine, I can stop worrying."

"Please. And also, don't tell anyone you know I'm alive."

"Why? Are you still in trouble?"

"I gotta go. Congrats on the new boyfriend."

Before Thea could ask any more questions, Aria hung up. Her brow furrowed.

"What's up, my little parakeet?"

"I'm trying to remember if I have a boyfriend."

Chapter Ten

Okay, so Constantine's vehement hissing might have been a little over the top. That did not excuse Aria's smirk and taunting, "Someone is jealous."

Indeed, he was, which made no sense. They weren't dating.

Yet.

Ever.

Ha.

Nothing worse than losing an argument to yourself.

"Are you ready to go?" he asked, lest he spend too much time trying to decipher the muddled state of his mind.

"I don't know if leaving right now is a good idea."

"I disagree. Hitting a few places you might have visited could trigger some memories."

"Or bullets. What if someone does want to kill me?"

"Then it will be a first date we'll both remember."

The words hung in the air, yet another clue that things between them weren't behaving like they should. He kept saying and doing things he'd never imagined. He got the impression she did, too. But they both covered it up.

"Come on, don't be a scared budgie. My truck's outside. Within ten minutes, we'll be in town and sitting down to eat." He saw the war of indecision flash on her face. "Come on, you know you want to go. What if you walk into the diner, and bam, you get all your memories back?"

"Exactly what kind of menu do they have?"

"They deep fry most of their seafood and have the best homemade fries and frothy shakes you ever sucked back."

The recommendation tilted the scales.

"Let's go. But I'm telling you right now, if I get killed because you miscalculated, I'm coming back to haunt your ass."

"If it's any consolation, if you do get killed, I'll avenge you."

She wrinkled her nose. "Not reassuring, angel."

But his feisty lady didn't protest any further, which was why they found themselves eating a short time later.

Or at least he ate. She picked at her food like a fussy bird.

"I'm done." She pushed her plate away.

He couldn't help but stare at it. "You only ate half of it."

"I know. I usually eat less than that, but I guess I was so hungry. And it was awfully good. I am so full that, even if I could sprout wings and fly, I doubt I could heave myself off the ground." Aria patted her belly.

"That is not a meal."

"Says the guy who's like twice my size."

"I'm eating it." No way would Constantine let good food go to waste. He couldn't help but notice she watched him, a hint of a smile on her lips.

"What's so funny?" he asked once he'd cleared her plate.

"You are. I don't know why you were complaining about my eating habits when it seems the leftover food was just what you needed."

"A man needs his energy."

"Energy to do what?" she asked with an arch of her brow.

A slow grin pulled at his lips. "All kinds of things." Things a man shouldn't think about doing with a woman he barely knew, who didn't even know herself.

"Let's make one of those things taking a walk downtown to see if something jogs my memory."

Constantine paid the check, but before he could slide himself out of the booth, he noticed Aria stiffen. "What's wrong?"

She leaned forward and lowered her voice. "That guy, the one at the counter. I know him. Or at least I recognize his face."

"Another memory flash?"

She nodded.

"Do you know who he is?"

Her shoulders lifted and dropped. "No idea. I only got a quick glimpse of him swigging a beer."

Constantine's gaze followed the man as he left the restaurant, brown takeout bag in hand. "I've never seen him before." He stood. "Let's go."

"Where?"

"To find out where he's going of course. He could be a clue to unraveling your memories."

They exited Bayou Bites into bright sunlight, just in time to see a bright blue smart car leaving the parking lot.

She couldn't help but shake her head. "Oh hell no would I get in that."

"Why not? I hear they're good on gas."

"I like the things I trust to be bigger."

No way could he stop himself from swelling his chest when she glanced his way. "Big is always better."

She might have snorted, but her cheeks also turned a lovely shade of pink. "In the case of cars maybe. No way am I trusting that tiny tin can to protect me," she noted as she followed him to his truck.

"Says the girl who rode a motorcycle."

"I ride a motorcycle?" she asked as he pulled open his truck door.

He grabbed her around the waist and lifted her inside. "Yup. Nice one, too, 1200 ccs."

"I wonder what it feels like to have all that power between my legs," she mused aloud.

Did she do it on purpose? He felt sucker-punched and slammed her door shut before getting in the other side.

She didn't look at him, simply pointed. "Get moving before we lose him."

"Patience, goose."

She smacked him in the arm. "Idiot."

He laughed.

"So how did you know I rode a bike?" she asked. "Or let me guess. Thea again."

"Actually," he commented as he pulled out of the parking lot and followed the blue car at a distance, "I saw your bike at the B&B before the fire broke out."

"You saw my baby? Where is it?"

"Baby?" he queried with an arched brow.

"You have your dog. I have my machine."

"I take it you flashed on your bike."

"He has a name."

"He?"

"Anything that vibrates my girl bits that well has to be masculine in origin."

"So what do you call him?" he asked.

She fidgeted in her seat. "I don't remember."

Lie. He prodded. "Yes, you do. What is it? Tell me."

"Laugh and I will hurt you," she advised.

"Hurt me anytime you like, oriole."

She rolled her eyes, but he noted the hint of a smile curving the corner of her lip. "It's Fred."

"Fred? Who the hell calls a bike Fred?"

"I do, and I'll have you know it's short for Sir Frederick Full Throttle."

He couldn't help it. He snickered. Snorted. So she punched him, hard as she could in the space of the truck cab. As if it stopped him. He barely felt it. "I've had mosquitoes hurt me more," he teased.

"You want pain, I'll give you pain," she

muttered.

She placed a hand on his thigh.

He tensed. And he wasn't talking about his muscles, but rather a certain part of his body with a mind of its own.

She danced her fingers closer to his package, his noticeably bulging package.

"What are you doing?" he asked, switching his gaze between the ass end of the car he trailed and Aria, who sat staring at him, eyes shining bright.

"Hurting you."

Shit, she was going to sack him. Her hand moved, and he might have swerved as he prepared for the pain…of pleasure?

His breath caught as she cupped him, the heat of her palm branding him even through his denim.

Tell her to squeeze it.

This was one time his other half totally had the right idea.

Aria had her own, though. It involved rubbing him, back and forth, a heated friction that made him ache.

"Yessss." Excited, he couldn't stop the sibilant hiss.

She squeezed him. Held him. Drew his breath in fast pants and—

"Don't stop," he exclaimed as her hand moved away. He shot her a glance and noted it primly folded in her lap.

"Oh, I am stopping. But let me ask you, how are your balls?"

Heavy and aching and… He opened his eyes

wide. "That was just mean."

"I told you I'd get you back."

Flipping his gaze forward, he set his lips in a line, not amused at all by her laughter. How could he laugh when he might die because his poor balls and cock wouldn't be able to stand the disappointment?

"Are you sulking, angel?"

"No, my toucan."

"My nose is not big."

No, damn her, it wasn't. It was cute and tiny, with a tilt at the end.

"So whatever happened to my bike?" she asked, pretending as if she hadn't almost gotten them killed in a crash by sending all the blood in his brain south.

"I'm not sure. I don't think it got damaged in the blaze, but more than likely, someone towed it. I could find out if you'd like." Although why he offered, given her cruelty, he couldn't have said.

"I would like." She leaned forward. "Hey, where is our dude going?"

The small car turned off the main highway onto a side road. "Looks like he's staying local." Interesting, given Constantine didn't recall ever seeing the guy. The town wasn't huge, but it didn't take long to recognize most people. Then again, as the world got busier, so did their town. It wasn't as if Constantine went out much.

"What's in that direction?"

"Not much. A few houses and Bittech. He could be an employee there."

Except the guy drove past the turnoff for the

medical facility and kept going. They followed him several miles out of Bitten Point until he pulled into a roadside motel.

Constantine drove past, not too far, before he turned around. He brought them close to the motel before parking on the shoulder. He debated their next move.

Rat-tat-tat. He drummed his fingers on the steering wheel.

"What are you doing?" Aria asked. "Let's go talk to him."

"If we do, we'll be tipping our hand that you're not just alive, but hunting down clues to your disappearance."

"Didn't we tip it when we went to the diner?"

"Yeah, but you gotta admit those deep-fried shrimp were totally worth it."

"I think we should go and talk to him. Even if I don't flash a memory, maybe he can tell me where we met."

Valid points, yet Constantine wasn't sure about it.

Given the violent happenings he'd encountered, did he dare risk the recently discovered Aria to possible violence?

Or am I hoping that, by not remembering, she'll stick around for a while?

It irked him to even contemplate he had an ulterior motive in staying back. Aria deserved his help.

"Okay, we'll go talk to him, but stick behind me until we know he's not armed."

Slapping the shifter into drive, Constantine crawled his truck through the parking lot that paralleled each of the motel units. He parked across the back of the small blue car, blocking its escape.

With another firm admonition to stay behind him, Constantine approached the peeling green door for room number seventeen. He knocked.

While he waited, he sniffed the area and frowned at what he found, or more like didn't find. Exhaust fumes, cigarette smoke lingering in the air, oil from a car a few rows down leaking from a blown gasket. He also smelled humans, mostly male, a few perfumed females. What he didn't scent were any animals.

No shifters had come this way, which made their friend inside human.

A curtain beside the door twitched, but the door remained locked. Someone was trying to avoid them.

Bang. Bang. Bang. "Open the door. I know you're in there. Don't make me open it for you." The flimsy portal wouldn't stop a determined boot.

"What do you want? I don't know you. Go away."

Aria, tucked behind, actually listening to his instructions, whispered, "Just kick in the door, would you?"

"And have the cops called on me?" he muttered back. "He'll open it." He stated it with more confidence than he felt. Louder, "I just want to ask you a few questions. About a girl you might have met at a bar a few days ago."

"Are you a cop?"

"Nope. Just a friend looking for some answers."

To his surprise, the door opened, only a few inches, the security chain pulling taut as the fellow put his face in the crack. "Why do you think I know anything? I'm just in town doing some work for a lab. I don't really know anyone."

Before Constantine could stop her, Aria inserted herself in front of him. "Do you know me?"

"You! Oh hell." The door slammed shut.

"I think that answers the question," Constantine dryly remarked.

Bang. Bang. Bang.

"Go away. I want nothing to do with her. Because of her, I got into so much trouble. I was lucky I didn't lose my job."

"What did I do?" she exclaimed.

The door pried open again as a single eyeball glared out. "As if you don't know."

"She doesn't." And Constantine was tired of the dude screwing with them.

Boom. While he might not want the attention kicking a door in might cause, snapping a feeble chain? No problem.

He shoved at the portal, sending the guy blocking it stumbling as he advanced into the shabby yet clean room.

"What's your name? How do you know Aria? Who are you working for?"

"I don't have to tell you nothing," the stubborn guy insisted. "I'm calling the cops."

A finger stabbed in the dude's direction. "I remember you now!" Aria exclaimed. "You're the guy I kissed outside the bar."

Wham. Constantine's fist stopped the guy from dialing 911—and he also wouldn't be doing any more damned kissing any time soon either.

Chapter Eleven

Aria couldn't help a bemused blink as Constantine laid Jeffrey—*that's his name*—out cold.

"What did you do that for?" she snapped, perusing the unconscious body with her hands on her hips. "Now how's he supposed to answer our questions?"

"He was going to call the cops."

"And it didn't occur to you to just take the phone away from him?"

"No, because I was too busy wondering why you were kissing a twerp like him."

She gaped at him. "Are you jealous?"

His nostrils flared. "Yessss." The word hissed from him. "But I don't know why."

Just like she didn't know why his jealousy pleased her. Another aspect of the crazy attraction between them. An attraction she needed to deny—at least for the moment. "His name is Jeffrey. He's a lab technician at Bittech."

"You remember him?"

"A bit. We didn't really talk much."

"Too busy doing other things?" Constantine growled.

"No, because I'd just gotten into town that day and was doing my best to chat with everyone at the bar. Jeffrey was there with a few guys from

Bittech, having some beers."

"So how did you end up kissing?"

Given she doubted Jeffrey was her type, she hoped it wasn't her dreaded slut side making do with whatever was close at hand. "I flirted with him. Nothing serious. I flirted and chatted with everyone there." Or so she vaguely recalled. The bartender made a mean martini. "I got him talking about his job, and when I found out he just worked there as a lowly tech, I was going to move on. Except…"

Jeffrey saw his chance to impress a girl fleeing, so he blurted out, "I know about the secret levels."

"What secret levels?" Constantine asked.

Aria visibly startled, not having realized she'd spoken aloud. "I don't know. I'm just repeating the parts I remember from the memory flash. He also said, 'there's weird shit happening at Bittech, and I'm not just talking about the lousy cafeteria food.'"

"Wes Mercer, who works there as a guard, is convinced they're up to no good as well, but we've never managed to find anything concrete. But Wes is still convinced. If there are secret levels, then that might explain Wes's conviction that things happen out of sight."

"Things done out of sight and secretively are usually a sign folks are up to no good. I recall being excited about this news. I don't know why, though. Why would I care what they're doing at a medical research facility?" Her nose wrinkled.

"Are you a news reporter?"

She shook her head. "I don't think so. And according to Cynthia"—who had called during lunch despite being told not to—"I'm kind of vague on what I do for a job."

"Maybe you're a secret agent spy."

He said it in jest, yet something about his words rang a bell. It just didn't trigger a memory. "I wish I knew why I was so interested in Bittech."

"It could be because they're a medical institute for shifters. The humans think they're researching the effects of bayou plants on human cells, but in reality, they're supposed to be researching the shifter genome, and they also provide fertilization for infertile shifter couples. But I say supposed to because we've begun to suspect it's not just research happening, but experimentation, too."

"You think they're the ones who jabbed me? But why? Why me?"

"Perhaps they thought you'd be an easy mark. Cynthia did mention you were orphaned. Perhaps they assumed no one would come looking for you."

How sad that she didn't have a family to care. *I have Cynthia and her folks.* The thought and certainty did warm her.

As Aria paced the motel room, she noted the door remained ajar. She kicked it shut lest someone walking by wonder at the strange tableaux. In order to clarify the memory, she recited it in point form aloud. "So, I met Jeffrey at the bar, where he bragged about his super access. For some reason, I needed to know more. I remember wanting into the institute, so I stole his access card."

Much like a femme fatale on screen, Aria had

lured the slightly tipsy fellow into the parking lot.
Once there, she feigned a sudden passion for him
that involved a lot of slobber, on his part, as he
mashed his mouth against hers. Shudder.

The poor sod thought he was getting lucky.
In reality, Aria groped him so she could steal his
employee keycard. Once she'd switched the card to
her own pocket, while keeping her lips clamped tight
lest a stray tongue visit, she pushed away from
Jeffrey and, with a high-pitched laugh, said,
"Goodness, but that was hot. You make a girl want
to forget she's saving herself for marriage."

While he stood there bemused, she'd hopped
onto her motorcycle and sped off.

"Did you go to Bittech that night?"

Her lips twisted along with her forehead as
she strove to remember anything past getting on her
bike. "I don't know. Everything after me leaving the
bar is a blank." Not entirely—she remembered also
wiping her arm across her mouth to wipe Jeffrey's
slobber. "Ugh."

"Why ugh?"

"Why is it that the only kiss I remember is an
awful one?" As a former slut, shouldn't she have
tons of hot-kiss memories?

"We can't have that."

Before she could ask what he meant,
Constantine drew her into his arms and kissed her.

Kissed sounded so trite, though. This melding
of their lips, the electrical spark that arced, and the
languorous heat invading her limbs was far more
than just a kiss. It was an explosion of her senses. A

knee-buckling and breathtaking foray into passion.

As his mouth caressed hers, she couldn't help but moan and part her lips. The access led to his tongue sliding into her mouth sinuously so that it could twine with hers.

She couldn't have said when her arms wound around his neck or when his hands cupped her ass. Hell, she wasn't sure of her own name at that moment and not because of the amnesia. The passionate inferno licking at her nerve endings made only one thought possible.

More.

Her body pressed firmly against his, yet she still wanted closer. How would it feel to press against him, skin to skin? Clothing separated their flesh. Wretched fabric. His height impeded her as well from rubbing against him as she desired.

A mewl of frustration left her, but he understood it, or he felt the same thing because he lifted her high enough that her legs could wrap around his waist, pulling her heated core against him. How decadent, the feel of her sensitive sex rubbing and glorying in the hardness of his erection.

Her back hit the wall, and he took a turn grinding against her. Her breathing stuttered as he applied pressure with his body against the part of her that longed for his touch.

And then Constantine was gone. One moment he held her, pleasured her, brought her to the edge of longing, and the next he set her down so she leaned against the wall.

Why?

She blinked open eyes heavy with passion to note the door to the motel hung open. Sunlight streamed in and showed her completely alone.

"Shit!" Where was Jeffrey? Probably trying to stay ahead of a chasing Constantine.

Flying to the door, she peeked out in time to note Constantine's hard pounding on the pavement had him almost within arm's reach of a sprinting Jeffrey, who ran full-out, screaming, "Help! Help!"

Help came from the most unexpected place. From the sky swooped a lizard, or at least that was how it seemed. The body had a serpentine feel to it, even with its two arms and legs. The skin appeared green and scaly, every inch of it thick with muscle. The leathery wings spanned wider than she would have thought possible outside a fairytale with dragons.

The flying lizard dipped, clawed hands outstretched. It shrieked an ululating cry.

Jeffrey happened to peek upwards, and she saw him blanch. He stumbled as he lifted his arms to cover his head.

The clawed fingers of the flying monster clasped Jeffrey's arms.

"Argh!" The blood-curdling scream brought a few people to peek out of doors. What must they think to see the thrashing legs of the man as he was lifted into the air by a creature that shouldn't exist, a creature that stole their clue and taunted them with a raucous caw of triumph?

While Aria didn't remember the beast, the sound triggered a deep shiver. And she could have sworn a voice whispered in her head, *Hide.*

She ignored the suggestion as she clambered into Constantine's truck. He jumped in a moment later and gunned the engine. "Let's get out of here before the cops show up and ask us questions."

"Not keen on explaining how a flying lizard stole the guy we knocked out?"

"With this many witnesses all claiming it, they'll be hard-pressed not to listen. And that's a problem. This brazen act is going to bring attention."

"Not our fault."

"It's someone's, though. Did you see the collar around that thing's neck?"

She shook her head. Addled by the kiss and stunned by the creature, she'd not noticed much.

"I've heard of those collars before. Daryl and Cynthia said the pair of hybrids they dealt with wore some. We think they're some kind of device to control the monsters."

"You think someone is making those creatures do these things. But why? I mean, why kidnap Jeffrey in plain sight?"

"Perhaps because they thought he'd become a liability."

She clasped her fingers together. "Am I a liability? Will it come after me next?"

"No."

"You don't know that." She couldn't shake a sense of trepidation.

"You're right, I don't, but I don't plan to let you out of my sight, so if it does try, it's going to have to go through me."

The declaration warmed, even as it sent chills. *I don't want him to get hurt.* "I'm putting you in danger."

He took his glance from the road to shoot her a hard stare. "You're not doing anything to me. I chose to help you. I still plan to. A little danger isn't going to make me run away."

"This is more than a little danger."

"What can I say? I do everything big." He tossed her a wink.

She bit back a smile. "So I'm beginning to see. Where to now?"

"I think you've had enough excitement for one day. We're going home. Princess needs me."

Princess wasn't the only one.

Chapter Twelve

As Constantine pulled into the crushed gravel drive in front of his house, he noticed not only his mother's car, but his brother's, too. Odd because Caleb usually worked during the day. What had brought him out for a visit?

Exiting his truck, Constantine had no sooner slammed the door shut when his mother, her rotund figure still dressed in her scrub outfit that she wore for her work at the seniors' residence, came flying out of the house.

"I killed it!"

"Killed what?" he asked as he rounded the hood of his truck to give Aria a hand, except she didn't need one, having already nimbly jumped to the ground.

"I killed a monster. Come see. He's in the yard."

Grabbing Aria's hand, Constantine followed his mother's excited wobble around the house until they entered the backyard.

An alien scent assailed him. Reptile, with a hint of wrong. Sickness, with a sweet, rotted tinge. And death in the form of blood, a giant puddle of it under a winged creature, but not the same one they'd seen at the motel.

This one was smaller. Much smaller. The

slight frame was covered in downy gray fur, no scales, yet the reptile scent pervaded.

"What is that thing?" Constantine asked as he approached his brother, who knelt by the corpse.

Princess took that moment to let out an excited yip and left her post beside the body to fly at him in a sideways gait that looked awkward but adorable.

Letting go of Aria's hand, he swept his dog into his arms. "How's my little princess?" he asked, giving her wiggly body a nice scratch.

Yip. He snuggled her to his face, his affection for his dog not something he hid.

"I'd mock you and your bonding moment, but I have to say your dog is growing on me," Caleb announced. "She's a damned good watch dog and the reason why Ma even knew this thing was here."

"Was my little princess a brave puppy?" he cooed, and she almost expired of happiness.

"More than brave," his mother replied. "I let Princess out when I got home from work. Next thing I know, she's barking like mad, and I look out to see this *thing*"—a moue of distaste aimed at it—"trying to catch our valiant guard dog. So I grabbed the shotgun and took it down."

Indeed she had taken it down with a fist-sized hole through its upper body. His mother didn't mess around when it came to ammo for her weapon. As she explained, "If I gotta protect myself from something big and stupid enough to mess with me, then I am making sure it ain't getting back up."

"Who's a good girl? Who is she?"

Constantine sang as he tickled his dog under her chin.

Wiggle. Waggle. Princess loved the praise. Aria, however, seemed less than impressed with his dog's impressive skills. She rolled her eyes before walking toward the carcass. He gave her credit for not flinching or throwing up. The thing sat on the bottom rung of the pretty scale. Limbs somewhat misshapen, its face a freakish meld of human and a few things, it seemed. Monkey and something else. The fingers were tipped in claws, much like the hooks of a rapier-type bird.

"It kind of looks like a flying monkey," Aria remarked as she tilted her head to the side to contemplate it. "You know, like the one in that *Wizard of Oz* movie."

"Again, you remember an old classic but not your life?" Constantine couldn't help but tease.

She grinned. "What can I say? I'm being selective about what I recall. Weird thing, I'm having trouble with my memories from about a half-hour ago." And, yes, she did wink.

It threw him for a loop. *Is she implying she wants another kiss to remember?*

"I've never seen anything like this thing before," Caleb remarked. "Whatever it is, I'm going to wager it's not natural. See its wings?" His brother stretched one out, the membrane unfolding and stretching taut. The wing appeared covered in leather skin, not feathers or fur. "The wings are just like those of that dino creature we killed a while back. The one that took Luke."

A scary time. The fear they'd all gone through when the little boy was kidnapped by the monster wasn't something Constantine wanted to relive. Thankfully, his nephew had emerged unscathed and the culprit was dead. However, they'd celebrated too quickly, given the abomination wasn't alone.

"Similar and yet not. As I recall, that thing had scales, not fur, and it was at least twice the size of this one."

"That's because I think this one is a child. A teen, actually."

At Aria's soft-spoken words, all eyes turned to her.

"What makes you say that?" he asked.

"Because I've seen it before."

Chapter Thirteen

The memory took her by storm.

The shove in her back propelled her forward, and she stumbled, her hand flailing out and grasping the metal rods of a cell door. Actually, she noted as she peered around, they were cages. Not very big ones either, just deep enough for the occupant to sleep stretched out.

Between the cages were spaces wide enough that, despite the arms stretching through, they couldn't touch anyone else.

The scrabble of claws drew her frantic gaze to the cage she clutched.

Fingers, half flesh toned, half pale gray furry tufts, clung at the bars. Big eyes, blue and wide with fear and panic, peered at her. The mouth, protruding from the face, rounded in an O, and the most horrible sound emerged from the mouth.

More horrifying than its appearance was the realization it was a child, a teen she'd wager, given the skateboarding T-shirt and surfer board shorts it wore.

"You are looking upon the next generation," a voice whispered by her ear. "And you'll get to be a part of it, too."

Unfortunately, she couldn't tell them any more than that. The scene unfolded itself in a blink within her mind, leaving her with the memory of the eyes, so sad behind the bars caging it. That creature still had some humanity left to it, but barely. This thing, lying dead on the ground? All monster.

It was decided to keep the body a secret for the moment, and not because they feared trouble if they brought it to the right authorities. Any creature attacking was fair game. In the shifter world, if someone had gone wild and posed a danger to others, especially humans and their love of discovery, then swift measures had to be taken. Usually permanent measures. Justice arrived on swift wings.

She blinked as the knowledge became available.

"I say we keep it to ourselves for now. Daryl's got a friend who might be able to look at it," Caleb told them.

"Do it. I mean, giving it to the friend can't be any worse than the one we stashed at Bittech. Maybe this time it won't disappear, and we won't get bullshit reports that what we found was a regular animal.

Bittech. Bittech. Bittech. Once Caleb left with the carcass, his mother in tow to stay with Renny and Luke, Aria found herself alone with Constantine. And his dog, a chaperoning Princess.

Chastity belts had nothing on that dog. Every time Aria got anywhere close to Constantine, the mutt wedged her way between them.

Being a man, he was oblivious to the game his dog played, but Aria recognized it, and she wouldn't let it get in her way.

Way of what?

Claiming Constantine.

What? She refused to think upon it. Not

when she needed to assert herself.

The maturity level in the room when her big angel left to use the washroom dropped considerably when Aria got down on her knees to growl at Princess. In her defense, the dog started it.

When he returned, it was to find Aria perched on a stool, looking perfectly prim and behaved.

"Did I hear Princess growling at something?"

Her lip twitched. "I think she saw a squirrel."

He eyed her askance, but didn't push it. Meanwhile, Princess shot her a glance, one that Aria thought said, *Thanks for not ratting me out.*

As if she would. Constantine would probably take his dog's side if she did.

"Want a cup of cocoa?"

"Sure."

As Constantine busied himself putting a pot of water on to boil, she leaned on the counter, steepling her arms so she could rest her chin in her hands. She watched Constantine move in the kitchen, light on his feet for a man his size.

She mused aloud. "So, I was thinking."

"Why do I feel that should come with a warning?"

"I'm not Cynthia. You're safe." The certainty that her friend was the one with crazy ideas stuck. As did the belief that Aria always went along and sometimes embellished those wild plans.

"I highly doubt I'm safe," he muttered, his back to her as he spooned the hot cocoa into cups.

What was that supposed to mean? "If you want out because of the danger, just say the word and I'll leave."

He whirled. "Don't you dare go."

"Okay, I won't. But you just said you don't feel safe around me. And you're right. It's not. It seems everything connected to me leads to monsters."

"I can handle the monsters. What I'm less sure about is how to handle you." Piece spoken, he whirled back to the mugs, pulling the whistling kettle from the stovetop.

She blinked a few times as she digested his words. What did he mean by handle her? Since she wasn't sure she wanted the answer, she brought their conversation back on track. "I'm noticing a common theme among my memories and the monsters. Have you noticed that everything keeps pointing back to Bittech?"

"I do, which is why I'm having a hard time believing it."

"Occam's razor."

"I know the term, but not what it means," he said, stirring the brew in the cups with a spoon.

"Simplest answer wins. In other words, don't try and complicate the truth. Maybe things keep pointing back to Bittech because they got complacent and, in turn, lazy about covering their tracks."

"It just seems too easy," he said as he slid a mug in front of her. "Think about it for a second. Considering how long these things have been happening, even if they were getting sloppy, I find it pretty odd that all of a sudden events are escalating to the point they're not even trying to stay hidden. Monsters out in daylight. Dead bodies. People missing left and right. And wouldn't you know all the blame seems to be centering on the one company authorized to do legitimate research on shifters."

"I think it's a great cover. I mean, they have access to medical supplies, personnel, even blood work and other tissue samples. Is it so farfetched to think that underneath the veneer of legal activities, nefarious ones are also occurring?"

Hands wrapped around his mug, he nodded. "True. I mean, who would suspect a shifter-run installation of being so crooked? I guess I just don't want to believe that a company with our folk working at it would do something like that. I mean, for fuck's sake, Daryl's brother-in-law is the CEO's son."

"Has Daryl talked to him about it?"

"Yeah. And so did Wes, the guard who works there. Andrew claims they're not doing anything that hasn't been sanctioned by the SHC."

"Sanctioned?" She frowned. Something about that niggled. "Are you sure they've given their approval and just what that approval is for?"

The question should have proven an easy one, yet Constantine opened his mouth then shut it, taking a moment to think. "You know what, I don't know that anyone ever truly asked them. I mean, Pete told us they wanted us to back off, but then again, turns out Pete's son was involved, so his info is now suspect. As for the rest, other than Andrew's claim, my sources all got this second and third hand."

She swallowed the rich, sugary brew before replying. "So shouldn't we call someone on the SHC council?" Her mind blinked, and she saw herself in a hallway, the carpeting dark blue and almost new, the walls a muted gray. An older fellow grasped her arm to pull her aside and whispered, "Remember, tell no one. Trust no one. Report only to me."

Who is he?

Constantine shot a frown in her direction. "One does not just call up the SHC and question them."

"Maybe someone should."

Setting his cup down, he scrubbed a hand through his short bristles. "The last time someone did, they went missing. Wes's brother tried to do something about the shit happening, and he vanished into thin air."

"People don't just vanish."

"They do sometimes in the bayou," was his ominous reply.

His phone rang, a shrill old-styled ring that filled the ominous silence his words had wrought.

He glanced at the lit display. "I gotta answer this."

She took another sip of the cocoa as she peeked out the window. Constantine paced away from her and spoke in low tones to whoever called.

The sensation of something just out of reach plagued her. Something that she'd learned niggled. The answer seemed close, so close. If only she could find and pull the thread that would unravel the mystery in her mind.

"I gotta go out for a bit."

She returned to the present. "Where do you have to go? Who was that calling?"

"The fire station where I work. A body was found in a tree in the swamp. Since it might be shifter-related, I got called in."

"What am I supposed to do while you're gone?" Aria would never admit it aloud, but the thought of staying alone in his house, with the swamp that hid so many dangers nearby, did frighten her. She wasn't sure what her strengths were in a fight.

Poison.

What?

This odd, disembodied voice talking to her every so often really freaked her out.

"Angel, is it normal to hear voices in your head?"

Her out-of-the-blue question narrowed his eyes. "Depends on how many of them are telling you to kill someone."

Her lips pursed, and she glared. "You are not amusing, dickwad."

"Is it wrong to like that name better than the emasculating name of angel?"

"You'll be my cutie patootie angel in front of your buddies if you don't answer me. Do you hear voices?"

"Me? When did it become a question about me?" As she leaned toward him, practically snarling, he laughed. "Yes, I hear *a* voice. Emphasis on the single entity who feels a need to chat me up sometimes."

"So your snake does talk to you." Winner for strangest conversation of the year.

"Talks, thinks. When our animal side is taking a backseat, they're more or less dormant. They will awaken for extreme emotions or because of a sixth sense when it comes to danger. They also like to meddle and throw in their two cents."

"By they, I mean it, or is that he?" Her brow furrowed. "Whatever the fuck is inside you, it doesn't make you kill things?"

Constantine might have joked before, but now he looked utterly serious. He braced both palms on the kitchen counter and angled closer. His intent stare locked her eyes on him.

"Aria, is something telling you to kill things?"

"Not exactly. A voice just told me I use poison."

"Told, but you didn't see yourself actually doing it?"

"No."

"That's not exactly solid evidence of anything then, is it?"

"Except it sounded true. Felt true. I poison things." She slumped. "And here I was hoping I secretly had some cool judo moves I could use in case someone came to attack me."

"You won't need cool moves because I'm dropping you off somewhere safe while I check things out."

Somewhere safe being with Cynthia and Daryl.

Chapter Fourteen

As Constantine drove away, leaving Aria at the tender mercy of her best friend, who clutched Aria to her bosom swearing she'd never let her out of her sight, he couldn't help but chuckle remembering the words Aria threatened.

"I will poison your beer."

What could a man reply to such a dire threat?

"If I can't drink, then I'll need to do something with my lips. See you later, my little peacock." Wink.

And then he fled. He'd probably pay for that later. He could see Aria getting even for leaving him with Cynthia, who exclaimed, "Have you put your toes around his ears?"

Not yet, but he hoped his little bird would soon. Damned woman turned his world topsy-turvy. She made him want to be the man his father wasn't, a man she could count on.

Crazy thinking. The kind of crazy you got from sniffing gas for too long.

He barely knew Aria. A man didn't suddenly want a commitment with a girl he'd just met, who didn't even remember who she was.

Don't forget Princess hates her.

Then again, Princess hated almost everyone. She tolerated his friends. She kept trying to get between him and Aria, though.

Should he take it as a sign?

Thing was he didn't want to keep his distance. Couldn't. Even now, dumping Aria off to go to work irked him.

He wanted to spend more time with her. Getting her to talk, he enjoyed discovering piece by piece the different fragments that comprised Aria.

The more he saw, the more he liked. Yet, that like kept distracting him.

I almost got her killed today.

An exaggeration, but a possibility given what happened to Jeffery. What if the winged beast had grabbed Aria instead? What if that furry flying monkey at his house today had done more than piss off his dog because it wouldn't land for a proper terrorizing?

Ma killed it. Bu, as he'd seen today with the flying thing, whoever they stalked had more than one creature at its command. They were also getting more brazen about using them.

Once the monster comes out from the closet, can you really shove it back in?

The answer terrified him in a way nothing else in his life ever had.

What if the human world found out about them? Scholars in the shifter world had long theorized that humanity might accept them, but even if the majority did, there would always be a faction who didn't trust *the animals.*

A mob usually started with only one cajoling voice. Just like it took only one bullet to end a shifter life.

Dark thoughts that led to carnal.

How? Because if their very existence hovered on a precipice where tomorrow could see them exposed and hunted for extermination, then he should seize the day. *I should seize Aria.*

Take her. Hug her. Squeeze her.

Or he could destroy the monsters and find the one controlling them. Take that danger out of Aria's life so he could take his time with her.

Snort.

Why not do both? Help save his town, save his ladybird, and maybe attempt something his father never did—a happily ever after.

He'd think on it. First he had work to do.

The trip out to the murder site didn't take long since he went there direct. He joined several others of his shifter brethren who also worked with the fire department for Bitten Point.

Luckily, only a few humans, which they couldn't avoid hiring due to labor law, also worked with them. In cases such as these, with a suspicious dead body, they were conveniently left out of the rotation.

People thought it odd the fire department showed on so many scenes that didn't even have a trace of smoke. People tended to think of them only in terms of fire. Except firemen, especially in smaller communities, played a larger role.

They also had the tallest ladders.

As Constantine braced the ladder for his buddy, Mick, he peeked around. The scene where he found himself was actually not quite in the swamp, the land firm and dry under his feet. The copse of trees growing wildly here sat on federal land and wasn't open to anyone but game officials.

So how had someone spotted the body?

"No Trespassing" signs proved the irresistible lure for teenagers. Dragging a girl by the hand, and saying they'd protect them from crocs and snakes, many a teenage boy got lucky in these woods.

Not poor Boyd. Poor Boyd had been lying atop Steph, doing his best to score a home run when his date started screaming—and it wasn't because of his technique.

As it turned out, opening her eyes while he nibbled on her neck and shoved a hand up her shirt wasn't enough to stop poor Steph from noticing a dead body hung in the branches of the tree overhanging them.

It put a damper on the date, for Boyd at any rate. Steph, just a few steps out of high school, was twirling her hair and chatting to the young policeman who showed up on the scene wearing an impressive badge and a gun.

Mick clambered up the ladder and muttered his findings, not too loudly, as he knew Constantine would hear him.

"It's male."

"Dead or alive?" While pretty sure it was the former, it never hurt to be sure.

"Definitely dead, but not for long. The blood is still fresh. No sign of rigor yet either. Poor bastard, I hope he died quick after whatever got him tore his face off."

No way could Constantine suppress a wince. That had to hurt. "Any identifying marks? Do we know who the victim is?"

"Fingers are gone. Chewed off it looks like. Damn, whatever did this to him, it's almost like they didn't want us to identify him."

Except once Mick untangled the body and eased it down to Constantine, he realized he knew who it was. He recognized the shirt.

Jeffrey. Last seen in the claws of a winged lizard. Now dead. Fuck.

Once the body left the branches of the tree, it was up to the cops and other crime scene dudes to take over—taking evidence and suppressing it in case it raised too many flags.

Since his services were no longer needed, Constantine didn't stick around. *I have somewhere else I should be.*

And as much as his python wanted that to be by Aria's side, that wasn't his destination.

If he assumed the winged creature had targeted Jeffrey specifically, then that meant the dead Bittech employee knew something.

I had him in my grasp. Dammit. If only I'd not let him escape.

If only he'd not kissed—nah. He wouldn't regret the embrace with Aria. Hell, if he'd known ahead of time Jeffrey would get snatched, he might never have stopped.

Thinking of Jeffrey proved sobering, though. The man was dead. Killed. But why? What did the guy know, and of more interest, did he perhaps write something down? Could there be a clue in his things?

I need to search his room before the cops identify the body and get to it.

Despite breaking a few speed limits, Constantine made it too late to the motel.

"Fuck." He couldn't help but mutter an expletive as he noted the billowing smoke obscuring a twilight sky.

Given cop cars blocked the road, along with fire and news trucks, he parked on the shoulder and walked the rest of the way. He couldn't get too close to the scene of the fire—they had the area cordoned off—but he stood amongst the crowd, a spectator that watched the hypnotic leap of bright flames.

The motel burned, and to his trained eye, he could already tell there would be no saving anything.

"Any idea how it started?" he asked a fellow beside him.

"Started in room seventeen. I should know, I was right beside the damned thing when the alarms went off. Weird thing, though, was the room was empty on account the guy staying in it got grabbed by some kind of giant bat."

Bat? Had to love how the humans wedged the truth into whatever box fit it best.

Since this wasn't his jurisdiction, Constantine got to watch as others put out the fire. He probably shouldn't have spent that much time getting hypnotized by the destruction, yet he couldn't help himself.

For one, it was warm and his snake did so like the heat.

Second, he needed the heat because the very act of arson made his blood run cold. Things were snowballing, and he feared how far they would go. And who else would die.

This violent act only served to reaffirm his conviction that time drew short. At the rate the blatant acts happened, and in front of witnesses, discovery seemed imminent. Death and injury were becoming commonplace. His time and window with Aria could find itself limited.

He should go to her and continue that kiss they began. Bring it to its rightful conclusion.

He choked—ironic really, given as his python usually choked others. But the thought of taking things to the next level terrified him.

What if I'm just like my dad?

Aria was an orphan. Could he give her a family only to yank it away because his snake got bored?

You never left Ma.

True, yet with Ma there was no pretense or expectation. She'd love him no matter what. He could do no wrong—unless he accidentally left the seat up and she fell in the toilet in the middle of the night. He paid for that with starched laundry.

You would never abandon Princess.

Of course he wouldn't because she loved and relied on him. He had a duty to protect, care, and adore her in return.

Couldn't you do the same thing with Aria?

Why not? Constantine usually took his duties seriously. Just because his dad had left didn't mean he would be the same. He'd proven himself reliable so far. Why would he suddenly change?

I am not making a decision about Aria and the future yet.

He had better things to do, such as make a pit stop to see Wes, his brother's frenemy. Personally, Constantine didn't have a beef with the guy. He seemed nice enough. Not his fault Wes bore that bad luck name—Mercer.

Everyone knew the Mercers, the family whose name was usually spoken with a condescending sneer. In some respects, they deserved it. A good number of Mercers tended to skirt the law or outright flaunt it.

Yet others, like Wes and Bruno and a few other Mercers, did try to live the straight and narrow. Not that it mattered in the grand scheme of things. Born a Mercer, always a Mercer.

Constantine felt kind of bad for Wes. The guy got a bad rap because of his birth, not his actions, kind of like his snake.

But becoming bosom buddies wasn't why he popped in to see Wes. He wanted to update him on the newest aspects of the case. A phone call might have proven quicker, but paranoia had him wondering now if those were safe to use.

Someone seemed awfully well informed about their movements. Did someone spy on them? The movies certainly made it seem like it was easy.

Ironically enough, he went looking for Wes at

his place of work, Bittech. Despite more or less running the entire security division, Wes still liked to rotate his shifts around, supposedly to keep a feel for staff and goings on.

As Constantine pulled into the front of the mirror-glass-plated building, he shut off the engine. He wanted to hear if anything approached.

The bright security lights proved harsh, their fluorescent glow bathing things and giving them a stark, dead appearance. Wes, however, didn't stand under its bright glare. Gators were nocturnal creatures for the most part. Nasty bastards, too, if riled. The big guy, a rival for Constantine's own bulk, leaned against the building, the red tip of his cigarette pinpointing his presence.

Nasty habit and one Constantine didn't get. Fire and smoke were a shifter's worse enemy—other than discovery. Why would anyone intentionally inhale the shit?

"What was so important you couldn't talk to me on the phone?" Wes asked, grinding out the butt under the heel of his dull black combat boots. They should have looked out of place with his pressed slacks and dress shirt, but then again, that dress shirt had two buttons undone, the tie hung loosely, and Wes, no matter how much gel he put in his unruly hair, would never look quite respectable. None of the Mercers ever did.

"I saw one of our friends today."

The slouch disappeared as Wes straightened and fixed him with his dark gaze. "Which one?"

"The flying dino. I saw it clear as day when it

swooped out of the sky. It attacked some dude I'd gone to visit."

"It actually attacked?" Wes's voice pitched almost as high as his brows.

"I didn't see the attack part, more like the kidnapping. Damned thing plucked him off the ground and took off with him like he was some kind of mouse. Some kids found the body in a tree. It wasn't pretty."

"Who was he?" Wes asked sharply.

"One of your Bittech fellows by the name of Jeffrey."

Wes's brows drew together. "Former employee. He was canned almost a week ago for compromising the institute's security."

"Lost a key card, did he?"

"How the fuck did you know that?"

Explaining Aria would take too long so he summarized with, "A little birdie told me. Anyhow, the flying lizard thing didn't just take off with Jeffrey. He tore off his face and fingerprints, too. I only recognized him because of his clothes."

"The monster has gotten a taste of blood. That's not a good thing," Wes noted.

"No kidding. I also don't like the fact that it's hunting in daylight."

"I wonder where it's holing up in between sightings."

"No idea. He seems to poof in and out of thin air. Without tracks, he's impossible to follow. Lizard thing wasn't the only weird monster spotted today. Another one visited my house. Ma killed it."

He couldn't help the pride in his words.

"Another lizard creature?" Wes barked.

"No. This one was more like a mutant flying monkey. Weirdest fucking thing I ever saw. Covered in fur, not scales. This one had quite the tail, too. A long, whip-like appendage with a barbed end."

Wes struck a match and lit another cigarette. He took a long pull before asking, "Did you bury it? Or feed it to the gators?"

"Neither yet."

"Good plan. We need to study it for clues. We can use it as proof to the SHC that there's shit going on."

"I think there's more than enough proof at this point for us to admit that the High Shifter Council doesn't give a rat's ass."

"Are you saying you're just going to give up?" Wes blew the question out as casually as the rings of smoke.

A snort escaped Constantine. "Like fuck. I can't. There's still at least one more lizard creature out there, murdering folks. We still don't know for sure dogman is dead." He shook his head. "I can't stop. Not until I know we've taken care of all the people, or things, involved. I need to keep Aria and my family safe."

Wes paused, hand suspended in air, the glow of his cigarette jutting from between his fingers. "Keep Aria safe? I thought that was the girl Cynthia said was missing."

"I found her. More like she found me. Anyhow, I'm kind of keeping an eye on her on account she lost her memory and she can't remember if anyone is out to get her."

A dark brow kept rising until Wes finally said, "Have you been sniffing swamp gases? Or has the group been keeping shit from me? No one told me she'd been found."

"Things were kind of hectic, and Aria was really adamant I not tell anyone about her."

"Too late now."

Very true, so Constantine laid the whole thing out for Wes, except for the kiss. That he kept private.

At the end of it, Wes lit yet another cigarette.

This time, Constantine felt a need to say something. "Are you trying to make yourself into smoked gator meat?"

Acrid smoke blew into his face. "We'll all die someday. Some of us sooner than others."

"Whatever, dude. Anyway, I should head back to Daryl's and grab Aria and Princess."

"You staying at your place?"

"I don't know. I was thinking of getting a room in town. The house is pretty isolated, and while Princess is pretty tough, she is small."

"What of the woman?"

"She's pretty tough and small, too, but she knows how to hold her own." And for the things she couldn't handle, he'd be there to help.

"Don't tell me she's got you whipped already?"

"Nothing wrong with a guy getting serious about a girl."

"Until that girl leaves you because you're not good enough. Women are trouble. It's best to steer clear."

Constantine had to wonder as he drove away just who had crushed Wes's emotions to the point he sounded so bitter. The only girl he'd ever really seen the guy serious about was Melanie, but it had been years and years since their breakup. Hell, they'd both been kids in high school still.

As Constantine drove, he broke a few laws regarding speed and texting while driving. Yet, it was worth it, given the enthusiastic way with which Aria flung herself out the door, Princess at her heels, waving a hand over her head while Cynthia yelled from the door, "If those toes go anywhere near his ears, I'll expect details."

As Constantine came around the front of the truck, his heart rate accelerated. Enjoyment at seeing her inflated him with warmth. It didn't help that she smiled as if pleased to see him.

Ours. We should hug her and squeeze her.

Or he could take the cowardly route, drop to one knee, open his arms wide, and exclaim, "Where's Daddy's sweet baby girl?"

Mock him and die.

The babbled words were totally worth the sight of his dog careening at him with her lopsided gait, tongue lolling as she emitted happy yips.

"You hate the name angel, yet you don't think that display is emasculating?" Aria couldn't hide her sarcastic lilt.

"Nothing wrong with a man's love for his

dog. Jealous?"

He peeked at her as he scooped his dog into his arms.

She might have spat, "No." But this close to her, he could hear the patter of her heart, a rapid thump. Even odder, he could swear he felt her disappointment.

Perhaps he had sniffed swamp gases because, in the next second, he stood and pressed his lips against hers, a fleeting kiss before pulling away, and with a grin, he said, "How's my fluffy-wuffy little swan?"

Instead of taking offense, she stepped into him and, reaching on tiptoe, nipped the tip of his chin, and growled, "Hungry."

Unfortunately, she meant for food. Real food.

And where could a guy take his gal late at night with his little dog where they served great food and didn't ask questions?

The Itty Bitty, of course.

Chapter Fifteen

Nothing like taking a girl who barely needed a bra to a strip joint, with giant, bouncy boobs all over the place. It made Aria feel somewhat inadequate in the chest area. She took her irritation out on Constantine.

"I can't believe you brought me here." Seriously, he didn't seem like the type who went to the nudie bar.

"I know how it looks," he muttered, his fingers laced through hers as he weaved her between the tables. "But trust me when I say the food here is excellent, the discretion top-notch, and besides, Renny works here, so I get a discount."

Was the food the only thing he got a discount on?

Shoving the irrational jealousy away, she tried to keep an open mind. After all, Aria knew stripping could provide a decent income.

How do I know that?

Shit, don't tell me I'm a stripper?

She really wished she could remember what her job entailed before coming to Bitten Point on her supposed road trip. Thinking about her past, though, resulted in a shushing sound, as if her own mind forced her to forget.

"Let's grab this booth at the back."

Constantine gestured to the U-shaped seating area, which, to his credit, sat farthest from the stage.

Before Aria slid in, she couldn't help but ask, "I am not going to stick to it, am I?" Nothing worse that getting glued to a foreign piece of furniture by unidentifiable globs. She refused to even entertain the thought of what those globs could be in a strip joint.

"This place is cleaner than most bars, actually. Much like snakes, exotic dancers and their places of work get a bad rap."

His words definitely put Aria in her place and also reminded her that she wasn't one to stick her nose in the air. She wasn't any better than anyone in here. From the bits and pieces she recalled, she'd done things she shouldn't take pride in. Funny how some of those same things people disapproved of were acts she still remembered with fondness.

"What are you ordering? I'm starved."

He cocked a brow at her. "I don't think they serve three chicken wings and seven and a half fries."

"Ha. Ha. What a funny guy. See if I share any of my leftovers with you now."

"Ah, come one. You gotta let me have them. You can't let good food go to waste." Then the big, dumb idiot batted his lashes and grinned.

He looked so bloody stupid and absolutely gorgeous at the same time. "You're whacked."

"Only with you. Most of my friends think I'm kind of dry with the humor."

"Or they don't understand it. That happens

to me a lot."

Reaching out, he snagged her hand. "This is going to sound dorky, but I'll blame it on hunger. I kind of like you"—his lips stretched—"bluebird."

"I'm wearing pink. And I like you, too." In what was the most awkward conversation ever. Since when did a guy hold her hand and try to look in her eyes as he claimed affection? Or was there another reason why he was acting so sappy?

"Are you stoned?"

He frowned. "No, why."

"Because this is weird, angel. Guys don't profess emotions in a strip joint."

Turning his head from side to side, Constantine surveyed the room. "What's location got to do with it?"

Aria couldn't help but giggle. Sincerity rang in his words. He truly didn't grasp the oddity. But she let it pass. Until he said, "So, I feel I should tell you right up front that, if we do take things further, I can't promise anything more than a casual thing. We snakes don't have a good track record with sticking around."

"So you're asking me out and breaking up with me all at once? How does that work?"

"I wasn't breaking up with you. And, I, um, didn't realize we were dating."

"Just because I might have been a slut in my other life doesn't mean I am going to be in this one. So if we're going to be making out on a regular basis, then I should at least be your girlfriend." Because then she wouldn't be a whore. She'd just be doing what she had to in order to keep her man happy.

He blinked. "That was confusing, but from what I think I understood, you're my girlfriend."

"Well, I thought I was, but then you broke up with me by saying snakes leave."

"We do. At least my dad did. It's something genetic about our kind. So even though I kind of really like you, it could be that some switch in my head turns off at one point and I'll just pack my things and go."

"Go where?"

Again, he regarded her for an instant. "What do you mean go where? Somewhere. I don't know exactly. Just that it might happen."

"Why?"

"Why what?"

"Why are you going to leave me?" As she asked, a woman dressed in black yoga shorts that hugged her every contour with a tight T-shirt and a large tray arrived at their table.

"Hey, Renny," Constantine said, relinquishing his grip on her hand.

"If it isn't my favorite brother-in-law," she teased as she placed some plates in front of them. Several plates. "I ordered your favorites with a little extra for your lady friend." A curious gaze turned her way, and the woman waited.

"Shit. Sorry. Aria, this is Renny, Caleb's wife. This is Aria," he told the other woman, who, done serving them food and drink, tucked the tray under her arm.

Brown eyes perused her. "So you're the girl

that they were looking for. Glad they found you. I know when the lizard man took Luke, I was scared out of my mind for him."

"I don't know what took me." As Aria blinked, she faded out into a new scene.

Through woozy eyes, she could see a ceiling. White plaster with a few hairline cracks and one stain. Whose ceiling did she admire?

A turn of her head showed a wallpapered wall, the pattern faded.

A blink, and when she reopened her eyes, she noted legs. Strangely shaped legs in dire need of a shave. More like a lawnmower, given how thick the hair grew.

What the fuck? She turned her head and peeked upwards. She noted the towering shape of a dog on two legs. A fucking humanoid dog. It glanced down at her, but it didn't loll its tongue in a happy greeting.

The muzzle drew back over black gums, revealing pointed canines. A low, rumbling growl came from it. Ominous. Deadly.

Fly away.

She flung herself to the side, in an attempt to get on her hands and knees. She needed to move away from the weird monster.

She didn't go more than a few inches before a hooked foot sent her tumbling, and she only barely missed smacking her face off the floor. Before she could recover, she noted she was face to shoe, as in leather loafer.

"And where do you think you're going?" a voice asked.

"Help me." The words emerged weak, trembling, just like her body.

"Help, oh I plan to. You scared her, Harold, with that hairy mug of yours. Or is it your breath? Perhaps you should stop snubbing your nose at the milk bones I offer."

It took her slow mind a moment to grasp the man in the leather shoes spoke to the dog creature.

A rumbling sound filled the air. It held menace, and it drew a shiver of fear. It cut off abruptly with a sharp yelp.

"Tsk. Tsk. Bad doggie."

The acrid stench of burning hair revived her a bit more, but while her mind woke, her body remained sluggish.

"Would you open the fireplace already? We need to get the girl out of here before your mother notices she's gone. I had the devil of a time trying to get the sleeping agent in the cocoa. Last thing I need is for us to be caught. Although, if your mother does stick her nose in our affairs, then you know what will happen."

Grrrr.

Aria pushed to her knees, but wavered, the drugs still coursing through her system, her every movement weighted and laborious.

"Grab the girl."

The hairy thing called Harold hoisted Aria by the armpits, none too gently either.

"Lemme go," she slurred.

"Not today. Today you get to help us make history. Or you'll die."

Snap.

The fingers clicked in front of her eyes, and Constantine's worried voice said, "Aria, earth to Aria, come in, Aria."

"Sorry. I kind of wandered there."

"What did you remember?" he asked.

"Them taking me into some kind of secret tunnel through a fireplace."

"Who did? Who took you? Do you remember?"

She did, but did she want to admit what she recalled? It seemed so farfetched now.

"There was a shifter and a man."

Constantine leaned on the table, and even Renny crouched down to get in closer. "Do you remember their names?"

"Harold and…" Her brow wrinkled. "I never heard another name."

"Was Harold by any chance a dogman?"

She gaped at him. "Yes. How did you know?"

"He's the same one we talked about before."

"You didn't give him a name."

"Because I have a hard time equating a name like Harold to whatever that thing is."

She shuddered. "There is something very unnatural about him."

"What about the other man?" Renny prodded. "Can you remember any details about him?"

"He's an ass."

A snort blew past Renny's lip. "That describes too many men."

"Tall, but really gangly."

"Smell?"

Aria's nose wrinkled. "I don't know. I was so fuzzy at the time on account of the stuff they laced my cocoa with."

"Any other details?"

"Reddish blond. He wasn't dark-haired. But not much else. I mostly saw his shoes." Finely cut, buttery looking, hand-stitched shoes. She'd recognize them again if she saw them.

Hunger took over at that point. Renny left to take care of other clients, and they dug in, Constantine having three bites for every one of hers. But she savored those bites, closing her eyes in delight at the crisp crunch of the home-style fries and the tang of the lemon pepper on the wings, sweetened by a light lemon sauce. Then there were the corn tortillas with a cheese and spinach dip. She ate a whopping eight of those.

Constantine ate the rest—well, almost all the rest. He did sneak tidbits to Princess, who sat beside him in the booth.

"If I keep eating like this, I'm gonna be too heavy to fly," she said with a pat to her belly. She froze. "Holy shit. I said I could fly."

"Now you sound like Peter Pan. You always could fly. It's just that your subconscious is revealing these tidbits a little at a time."

"I prefer that to the in-living-color movies." Those took her out of the moment and proved jarring, but not as jarring as the floorshow.

A shrill scream erupted from across the room. In a flash, Constantine slid from the booth and stood before her, scanning the room.

Another scream, louder this time as a girl dressed in a plaid skirt and tied-off white blouse came running from the curtains at the back of the stage. She wasn't alone in making an appearance on the runway.

The fabric, hanging as a red velvet shield, came tearing down. A grand entrance for Harold, the dogman from her most recent recollection.

Holy shit, he is real.

And when his baleful glare turned her way, she swallowed hard because she knew to the depth of her being, *He's coming for me.*

Chapter Sixteen

While he might not mind a little fur, Constantine had to admit tonight's floorshow pushed that limit.

The hairy beast loped onto the runway, not even wearing a thong or pasties while the red and blue and white lights streaked and swerved, giving the creature a surreal appearance.

Dogman—because he just couldn't think of him as Harold—let out a howl when he glanced their way. Freakish paws/hands pounded its chest.

"What is he, part gorilla?" he mused aloud.

"Does it matter?" hissed Aria. "We need to get out of here."

"Why?" He didn't turn to peek at her, but he did ask the question.

"Because he's coming for us," she yelled as she ducked under the table.

A good place to hide if she didn't have him and Princess—his valiant dog who stood atop the table barking and bristling—to protect her.

Constantine braced his feet on the floor, spread his arms away from his body, and waited, timing his next move carefully. He grabbed dogman mid-leap and used the momentum to swing him away.

Crash. The loose table on the floor couldn't

handle the force of the body landing and it skidded before collapsing. The impact didn't stop the beast.

Harold, still wearing his collar and looking more rabid than a certain dog in a movie, sprang to his feet, ignoring the scattering patrons as they bolted for the exit.

Harold had eyes for only Constantine.

Good. Let the monster focus on him instead of the others. He flexed his fingers. He could use a bit of exercise.

With a sweep of his arm, Harold cleared a table laden with beer bottles. The tinkling breakage of glass brought a few stray screams from those still within the room. They, like Aria, chose to dive for cover instead of running.

Princess loved a challenge, and Constantine could only watch with bemusement as his dog bolted to within a few feet of Harold, where she proceeded to prance and bark madly.

Grawr.

As if that intimidated his dog. Princess squatted, peed, and then turned her back with a disdainful diss.

GRAWR! "Schnackk," Harold lisped.

The dogman spoke, and Constantine bared a smile. "No one's eating anyone today." Unless Aria was on the menu—a menu for him alone. "Forget about my brave Princess. What do you say you and I play, Harold? Does the big, ugly doggy who needs a bath want to play fetch?"

"That sounds like something Cynthia would say," Aria muttered from behind him.

Compared to a girl. His ego might never recover. As Harold ran at Constantine again, he revised his plan. Hand-to-hand with the rabid beast might not prove his best course of action. He didn't have the claws or slavering jaws the monster did.

Yet he wasn't one to swap into his snake without good cause, especially since there were still witnesses around. Snakes freaked people out. Didn't matter if he was the good guy here. People would see his python and scream, or try to kill him.

But he was less worried about that than the opinion of a certain woman.

Did he want to scare Aria?

That would solve the problem of me possibly walking away. Get her to leave first.

What a cowardly way of dealing with his fears.

As Harold once again leaped, front paws tipped in claws extended, he ducked and let Harold soar over his head to crash into the table behind him.

Aria squeaked, but scuttled out from under the table.

"Run," he advised. "Get outside if you can, into my truck." Where he hoped nobody waited for them.

Flipping around to face the really pissed-off dog thing, Constantine stripped off his shirt and put his hands to the button of his pants.

"Why the fuck are you stripping right now?" Aria yelled, not having run away as he told her to.

"Gonna unleash my mighty snake."

"That better not be a reference to your dick."

No, but he should note his cock was mighty, too.

As Harold scrambled from his awkward wedge between the banquet seating and the table, Constantine shed his clothes. *Yessss, rid yourself of that unneeded, unnatural skin.*

His head lifted and his eyes closed as he mentally called his python.

While his cold-blooded beast didn't often talk to him, not like wolves and cats that had noisy partners, they did communicate through feelings.

So he felt the cold satisfaction as his body rippled. Every molecule undulated, and moving in a wave, they gathered and reformed. Reformed into something different.

One limb. One slick and smooth body.

"Holy fuck!" his delicate lark yelled.

It might have to do with his impressive size. Long, so very long, with a defined pattern on his skin.

I am attractive. It was only right the female admired his traits.

But the mating would come after the battle.

The enemy was almost upon them. He held his serpentine body upright as his jaw unhinged, opening extra wide. He hissed, the sharp points of his fangs projecting.

The smelly-thing hit him, and he whipped backwards, the enemy atop him. Claws went to rip at his flesh, but got caught in the thick leather of his skin. Still, it did sting.

He sank his teeth into the creature, wishing his had poison like some of his cousins. But he had something almost as good.

His tail, often possessed of a mind of its own, rose from the floor and moved with purpose. It slithered across the back of the hairy thing then tucked around its chest, back around again.

The dog let out a rancid, hot puff of air. Definitely not dinner material, but good for a squeeze.

The coils of his body tightened around the dog thing. Clawed fingers dug at him, some piercing the skin. The pain served to only tighten him further, a crushing vise around the unnatural thing until it exhaled one final time and went limp.

Since there was no point in keeping the body trapped, the length of him uncoiled from it, letting the limp meat sack fall onto the floor.

Movement from the corner of his eye caught his attention. His head pivoted as his body rose higher, a tall stalk towering to give him a vantage point.

The female observed him. *His* female. She did not exude fear, not much at any rate. He slithered closer, bobbing down to peruse her. Her breath caught, but she did not flinch.

Not prey.

Not this one.

He circled around her, around and around until she stood amidst a loose mound of coils.

A fluttery touch against his skin as her hands came to rest on him.

"You're hurt," she said.

Words he understood but couldn't reply to. The tip of his forked tongue flicked forth, and now she did lean back ever so slightly.

That did not prevent him from tasting her skin. He would know her flavor.

Voices yelled from afar. Others appeared to approach.

She pivoted in her ring and regarded him. "Angel, you have to come back now. There're people coming."

Perhaps they would provide a cleaner repast than the foul one on the floor.

"You have to change. We can't know who's coming. You know your kind get a bad rap. I don't want them to shoot."

Bullets. Ripping, tearing holes. No. Those did not appeal. And it was cold in here. Time for a nap.

Constantine threw his head back and heaved a deep breath as he came back to himself.

Of course, there was no hiding a six-foot-plus naked man on the floor standing a little too close to the naked dog thing.

Thinking quickly, Aria doused him with beer from an intact bottle.

When questioned, he stuck to his guns with a slurred, "I don't know."

Chapter Seventeen

Aria couldn't help but laugh at Constantine as he drove them to his house. Princess sat on his lap, one eye cocked, watching for trouble—in other words, making sure Aria didn't put the moves on her daddy.

As for Constantine, he kept his gaze trained on the road while sporting a stern countenance.

"Oh, come on, it's not that bad."

He snorted. "Not that bad? I think neutering would have been preferable to you telling the cops I was stripping for you."

"I only said it to explain your nakedness." Because poor Constantine didn't have time to pull on his pants before the cavalry arrived.

"Men don't striptease."

"They do out in Vegas." She had a vague recollection of a very drunk Cynthia dragging her to a show where the men wore G-strings, leather chaps, and nothing else by the end of the show. Made her want to ride a cowboy at the time.

"They can do whatever they like out west. I don't strip."

"Why not?"

"It's weird."

He sounded so discomfited she couldn't help but tease. "Some guys make good money at it.

You've got a good body and some serious moves. I think you could make a killing taking it off and shaking that snake."

"Snake?"

"I'm sorry. Should I have said your python?"

This time, he couldn't hide the quirk of his lips, although he tried to remain serious. "I am not stripping for money."

"How about for free?"

"How about not at all?"

She needled him because it was fun. So often he seemed to send her off balance. About time she returned the favor. "You know that's not technically true, given you just did it in public, in front of not just me."

"Only because I had to shapeshift. My legs can't fuse together properly if I'm wearing pants."

"Ever thought of wearing a dress?"

"No."

"What if I suggested you wore a kilt?"

"I am not letting my junk hang loose under a skirt. I'll keep it in my pants, thank you."

"Speaking of junk…" She snapped her fingers. "You just reminded me of something I wanted to ask, but you were kind of busy at the time. Where does your worm go when you're in like snakeman mode?"

"Worm?" He shot her a glance.

"Would you prefer the term willy?"

"I'd prefer it if we dropped the topic. Or if you're that obsessed with my dick then, by all means, grab a handful. Or mouthful. I'm not picky."

She knew he expected his words to shut her up. Except it was more fun to say, "Maybe I will suck on it."

Nothing more empowering than being able to tease she might blow him and have him almost crash the truck into a ditch.

"You are a tease," he growled.

"Only if I don't put out."

He did better at controlling his swerve this time, but that didn't stop her laughter. "So why are we going back to the house? I thought you said it would be too dangerous," she mentioned as she took note of the familiar landmarks.

"We just got rid of one of their main players. We got rid of another this afternoon. At this point, we've weakened them and shown we'll fight back. And we've proven we can win. Whoever it is behind the attacks will want to regroup before striking again."

"You mean gather his troops so they can stack the odds when they come after us again. That's not exactly reassuring." She wrinkled her nose.

"If you wanted reassuring, you would have left town by now. But you, my brave hawk, crave a bit of excitement."

She thought she had until the attack in the bar. "I highly doubt that, seeing as how my first instinct was to hide under a table." In retrospect, her cowardice burned. But what could she have done?

Lit your drink on fire and tossed it at dog boy, Molotov style.

Hindsight sucked. Aria had gotten used to the

voice talking in her head. What she had a bigger problem with was the violence it usually encouraged.

I thought we liked to poison.

Among other things.

It was the other things that worried her. As did the fact they were getting closer to the bayou, which meant closer to his house, a bed, and then seeing what would happen.

Since the explosive kiss they'd shared, he'd admitted to liking her, but also the fear he'd leave her. Honest, if not easy to hear.

Meanwhile, she could admit she also liked him and feared him leaving her. A fine dilemma.

But is that really any different from anyone else when they first start dating?

Everyone suffered doubt. Everyone entered relationships with the best of intentions. Sometimes, love grew stronger over time, or so the romance books claimed. In other cases, the bloom of lust wore off and the little things nagged until couples split.

She'd seen it happen before. While Aria might not have a family of her own, she'd grown quite talented at observing the families of others.

Funny the things she remembered. Most of her early life seemed okay to access. It was the more recent stuff she had problems with still. The biggest problem of all being what to do with Constantine.

I haven't known the guy long enough to really be thinking about this seriously.

Yet she couldn't help it. Which begged the question, why? Other guys scratched an itch. She didn't worry about getting involved with them or taking advantage of their bodies. With Constantine, though, she worried.

This is a man who could hurt me. Not physically, but because he made her want to stick around for a while. Maybe give that whole, "hey, you're cool, let's hang for a while" thing a go.

Commitment. Not something she knew too much about. Not something she felt comfortable with.

For some reason, she just couldn't think of Constantine in terms of only once. With him, it would be all or nothing.

She'd nicely circled back to her main dilemma again, the one where she feared to jump because she might fall flat.

But if I don't take that leap, I cannot spread my wings to fly. Faith that she would stay aloft. Could she give that faith to Constantine? Did she dare take a chance, grasp what she could, and give what simmered between them a chance to fly?

Nothing ventured, nothing gained—a motto never more apt than now.

The headlights of his truck illuminated his house, their stark brightness reflecting off the dark windows.

He shut down the engine, and they both sat in the truck for a moment, listening to the sounds of the night. The steady chirp of crickets. The hum of mosquitoes. The ticking of a hot engine cooling.

The sounds of normalcy.

"What are we waiting for?" she whispered.

"The weird part is, if I say flying monkeys, it's actually the truth."

"I hope there's no more of them." Shudder. She definitely wouldn't watch the movie about Oz without remembering the mutant version.

"I hope so, too, and yet I keep wondering what other monsters might be out there that we haven't seen yet."

"You think there's more?"

"Yeah. And for all I know, they're waiting in the shadows." He drummed his fingers on the dash of his truck.

"That seems unlikely given the nightlife seems pretty noisy and active." The distant croak of a toad punctuated her belief.

"Or they've been lying in wait so long that no one is taking note anymore."

"Are you scared?" she asked.

It wasn't just Constantine who snorted. His dog did, too.

"I'm not scared for me, but I am worried about you. Maybe coming back here wasn't such a good idea. I mean, we're pretty isolated. If they attack en masse, I might not be able to defend you."

"I thought you said you didn't think they'd try anything until they regrouped."

"I've reassessed that belief."

She rolled her eyes. "Stop second-guessing yourself. They're either here or they're not. And going somewhere else doesn't mean they won't follow. The best way to know for sure if something lurks is for one of us to go outside as bait." No sooner did she say it when Aria swung open her door, but before she could hop out of the truck, Princess scooted across her lap, onto the running board, then leaped to the ground.

"Just had to one-up me again, didn't you?" she muttered as Constantine flung himself from the truck with a cried, "Princess, stay where Daddy can see you."

While he might show concern for his dog, he also showed some for Aria as he loped around the truck. He arrived in time to grab her and swing her to the ground.

She didn't move away, and he didn't remove his hands. They stood for a moment, bodies close yet not quite touching, staring at each other.

"I don't hear any monsters."

"I don't smell any either," he replied, his gaze unwavering. The air between them sparkled with electricity. His hands on her waist were firm. Dare she even say possessive?

He drew her closer.

Yip.

With a sharp bark of annoyance, Princess broke the stalemate, yet she couldn't break the anticipatory tension humming between them. Nothing could, short of an attack. But nothing lurched from the darkness to eat them. Nothing swooped from the sky to snatch them. They made it into the house, not far, before their lips met with a hard clash of teeth.

Given Constantine's height, she needed help to reach. His hands spanned her waist and hoisted her so that their mouths could meet.

Meet sounded so trite, though. It was more an explosion of hot breath, wet tongues, and frantic need.

She cupped his face, loving the feel of his skin as she sucked at his lower lip.

"I want you." The words rumbled against her mouth.

They made her shiver and only served to increase the heat invading her.

"I want you, too." The soft admission made him groan, and she found her back pressed against the wall as his mouth continued to devour. Or did she devour him?

Did it matter?

There was nothing stopping them now. Nothing to prevent her clothes from being ripped from her body. She was just as violent with his clothing, her hands pulling at his T-shirt until he yanked it over his head, baring his skin.

The flesh-to-flesh contact of their upper bodies had her sucking in a breath. Could skin sizzle?

It felt like hers did.

With a strength she admired, and a body she longed to worship—with her tongue—Constantine pinned her to the wall. A good thing he held her aloft because arousal liquefied her limbs. She trembled, boneless at his touch, her body aware of every sensation.

The unshaven edge of his jaw scraped across her tender skin, abrading and awakening it as he kissed his way over to her ear.

He nibbled it. *Oh my.* He sucked on the lobe, and she moaned. It seemed she had an erotic spot, and he exploited it with hot breath, tugs, and sucks until she panted and clutched at his shoulders.

Then he left the tender shell of her ear, his lips trailing down the column of her neck. He leaned back, using his lower body to keep her pinned as he kissed his way down to the valley between her breasts.

Keeping one arm anchored around her waist, he let his other hand roam. Slightly callused fingers cupped a breast, his thumb rubbing against the protruding tip. Her nipple tightened to an even sharper point.

It took some adjusting, him hoisting her higher on the wall, but the new height meant he could latch his lips around her aching peak.

She made a noise as she clutched at his head, with pants and moans urging him on.

Take it deeper into your mouth.

He did. He sucked her breast in, the heat of his touch exploding in her.

Gasping and squirming didn't mean he hurried. Oh no. He took his time torturing her poor nipples, first one then the other. The nubs tugged with his lips, his teeth nipping at them while his tongue swirled around them.

He drove her absolutely crazy with desire, enough that she gasped, "Stop teasing me and fuck me already, would you?"

"But I'm having fun," was his rumbled reply,

the words quivering on her skin.

"And I want to come." She didn't need to say on his cock. He understood, and it was his turn to shudder.

He still wore his pants, and he took a few fumbling, precious seconds to push them down. Then it was her turn to lose her bottoms, his hands rough in their removal, but titillating as proof of his excitement.

Once he bared her to his touch, he repositioned her against the wall, his hands cupping her ass cheeks while his lips scorched hers in a passionate kiss. It rendered her quite breathless. His shaft throbbed against her belly, hot and *alive.*

As arousal ran like liquid fire through her veins, she sucked at his lower lip, her entire being thrumming with excitement.

I need him so badly.

"I need you."

He echoed her thoughts as he drew his hips back and let the hard length of him bob up from where he'd trapped it under her body. He angled his hips far enough back that the tip of him teased.

He might have his hands full, but she didn't. She kept her legs loosely coiled around his waist as she reached down. She gripped his cock firmly, and he sucked in a breath. Stroke. Stroke.

She slid her hand on him, keeping the head of his mushroomed shaft rubbing against her core.

Her arousal moistened the tip of him, covering him in a glistening sheen that made the rub against her clitoris even more moan-worthy.

"If you don't stop, I am going to come before I get inside you," he growled, his fingers digging into her cheeks.

"Oh no you don't," she muttered. She pulled at him, inserting the head of his cock into her sex, but then couldn't get him any farther.

He locked his body, and she growled. "What are you doing?"

"You're tight."

"And you're big."

"Exactly."

He worried about hurting her? She took her gaze from their bodies and their intimate joining to see he held himself rigid, the cords in his neck tense and shaking.

"Don't worry about me, angel. I can handle a little thickness, and I don't mind a bit of rough." With those words, she grabbed him by the cheeks and drew him close that she might kiss him. As he relaxed, she tightened her thighs and, with a chuckle of excitement, thrust with her hips, sheathing him.

"Fuck!" The word burst from him and was swallowed, much like her sex swallowed him.

She nibbled the tip of his chin. "I think fucking is a good idea."

His reply was a steady, groaning rumble as he began to move his hips. He moved them slowly, too slowly for her level of arousal. In, slow and languorously, letting her feel every inch, then out, a slick retreat that had her sex clutching at him.

No, don't go.

Back in, the slick friction making her tremble.

She clung to him, digging her fingers into his flesh, making a high-pitched, breathless noise.

"So fucking tight and sweet. Hold me tight. I'm going to increase the pace."

Did he know telling her would just heighten her excitement?

Her legs locked him against her, and since he couldn't pull out as far, he thrust deeper, butting against her sweet spot. Then he rotated his hips. Swirl, thrust, push, rub. The intensity against her sweet spot put her on the brink. She practically sobbed the pleasure of it.

How perfectly they fit together. A man with size, strength, and, best of all, the ability to use his rigid shaft and stretch her oh so nicely.

"Fill me. Fuck me." She managed to suck in a breath to huskily beg.

He groaned, the low rumble vibrating her being.

Faster he moved, the thrust of his hips grinding his cock into her.

He was so hard. So thick. So fucking thick.

Even as she came, he remained thick, perfect. Her body exploded against and around him. Waves of utter bliss stormed through her, shaking every atom of her being and then returning to run over her again. And again.

Endless ecstasy as he kept grinding and pushing and...

He came. Fiery hot, he jetted into her, bathing her womb with his seed. Leaving his mark.

The moment proved so utterly perfect,

especially when he leaned his forehead against hers, his breathing hot and ragged. She understood the need to recover.

Explosive didn't even come close to describing the cataclysm of the orgasm. She should note she did remember sex. And that was all it was. Sex. Not this intensely passionate and intimate joining of not just their bodies but, dammit, their souls.

I thought I didn't believe in that kind of sentimental shit.

Not anymore.

He's mine.

Her words. No one else's.

But not everyone agreed.

Chapter Eighteen

The low, grumbling growl drew Constantine's attention away from the glorious after-sex lassitude he indulged in.

Making sweet love to Aria had proved even more incredible than he imagined.

How could any man want to walk away from this?

The question was a good one, but took a backseat to his dog growling. What had his Princess on alert? He didn't sense any danger. His sixth snake sense didn't tingle, yet his pup didn't sound happy.

"What's wrong, Princess?" As he asked, he firmed his grip around Aria and carried her to the washroom, where a shower sounded like an awesome plan.

A shower with soap, rubbing, and naked skin. Hell, yeah.

Grrr. Ruff.

Princess still didn't seem happy. Something perturbed her. Constantine stopped short of the bathroom and looked around, checking for signs of danger. Not sensing anything amiss, he peeked down at his dog, who sat at his feet, big eyes staring right at him.

"What is it, baby girl? Tell Daddy what's wrong."

"She's jealous, angel. I don't think your

Princess likes to share. And do you know what?" Her lips nuzzled the skin at his neck. "Neither do I." Chomp.

Aria bit down hard on his skin, so hard he gasped, his cock hardened, and his dog lost her shit barking.

He fell against the bathroom wall with a heavy thud.

"What the hell was that for?"

"Just proving a point. Princess thinks I'm dangerous and wants to take me out," she whispered with warm breath against his throbbing skin.

"I think Princess is right. You are dangerous. But then again, so am I." And his dog would have to learn to share him because he wasn't ditching Aria. "Princess, Daddy needs to take a shower to get clean."

"Oh no, it will be dirty," Aria promised.

Fuck. He couldn't stop his cock from swelling at her words. "Go guard the house. Be a good girl."

Yip. With a woebegone look in his direction, Princess slunk out the door, and he might have felt guiltier if he hadn't caught the dirty look his dog aimed at Aria, but he could understand the glare, given Aria murmured, "I win."

"No, I win, because now that I've got you wrapped in my arms, you can't escape."

"Why would I want to?" she asked.

"Because I'm going to do such bad, bad things to you."

She shivered. "Please do."

He would. As soon as he got some hot water to sluice them off.

Keeping her tucked against him, where she belonged—*hug her, squeeze her, never let her go*—he turned on the taps. The hot water tank was just behind the shower, not far, so that meant it didn't take long for the jetting droplets to warm.

He stood in the tub, putting her back into the hot spray.

She sighed and leaned back into it, exposing the smooth column of her throat, a gesture of trust among predators.

He nuzzled the skin, tempted to leave a mark of his own. But the moment wasn't quite right.

But I can make it perfect.

He leaned her back, forcing her back to arch, pushing her sweet tits into the air.

Absolutely mouthwatering. He freed one hand that he might run a finger around her breasts, tracing them.

She muttered a husky, "What are you doing?"

"Admiring the view."

She snorted. "You don't have to lie."

"What makes you think I'm lying? Does this feel like I'm lying?" He slid her far enough that she could feel the hard jut of his cock, already raring to go.

Her eyes opened then shut as the shower water got into them. "Ugh," she exclaimed.

He laughed and turned her, putting her sideways so her head could lean against the tub liner.

It didn't impede his view. It actually made it

easier for him to lean down and grab a tip with his lips.

She gasped, and her fingers clutched at his scalp. "I don't have big breasts."

"And?" He bit down on the nipple, causing her to dig her nails in for a delicious bite of pain to offset his mounting need.

"Just saying I don't have big boobs. Or much of an ass."

"And again, I say what about it? From my perspective"—suck—"they're"—squeeze of those cheeks—"perfect."

And mine.

All mine.

A concept that really was growing on him. Just like she grew on him. Usually, snakes shed unwanted epidermal layers, but this was one time he wanted to wear someone else like a skin. He wanted Aria to wrap herself around him. He also wanted to taste her.

Now.

Like this very instant.

"Brace yourself," he warned. He set her feet down on the bottom of the tub and made sure she leaned against it. He dropped to his knees before her, letting the weak spray of water hit his shoulders and roll down his back.

As he brought his face level with her mound, he parted her thighs.

A rapidly sucked-in breath drew his attention upward. He noted her watching him, biting her lower lip.

He didn't need to see her face, though, to smell her arousal. This close to her sex, he could scent it. It tempted him.

He brushed her inner thighs with the rough edge of his beard, scraping the bristles over tender flesh.

A shudder went through her. Another when he nosed at her, rubbing his face against her pubes, inhaling her scent. Her essence.

He imprinted her so that he would never forget.

I'll never forget. How could he when she smelled so deliciously woman? So decadent.

He lapped at her, a long, wet swipe of his tongue across her clit.

That brought the grasping fingers to tear at his hair.

Another long lick and she made the most beautiful mewling sound. But her clit was only one treasure to discover.

It took only a swipe of his tongue for her plump, pink lips to part for him. Her honey coated his tongue, drugged him with her arousal. How sweet she tasted. He needed more.

Lapping at her, he probed and teased her sex for a moment before returning to her clit and sucking it.

Captured by the pleasure he lavished upon her, Aria dug her fingers in harder. She clutched him so tight.

Yes, tight. So good.

He wanted to get crushed by her. The more

pleasure he gave, the tighter she got.

She also got wild, a little rough, her hips bucking and thrashing.

I like it.

And she liked it when he gripped her hips in his hands, his outdoor-tanned skin against her white flesh a pleasing contrast.

Mine.

Holding her fast, he lashed her with his tongue, and with her ability to buck gone, Aria moaned, loud and often.

When her body began to quiver, he knew he'd taken her as far as he could. She was ready for him.

In a swift motion, he stood. He caught her lips with his, sucking at the moaning passion, swallowing the sound of her pleasure.

His finger probed at the swollen entrance to her sex, thrusting into her, a finger fuck that had them both swaying their hips.

"Turn around for me," he ordered.

She did better than just that. She turned to face away from him, braced her palms against the wall, and thrust out her little ass.

And he ran into a dilemma. She was too fucking short to do it like that.

Fuck.

She peeked over her shoulder. "What are you waiting for?"

"A step stool to magically appear." He growled in frustration.

It took her less than a second to grasp the

problem, and the minx laughed. "Poor angel. I guess we'll have to get innovative."

Apparently, her idea of innovative involved her streaking wet and naked out of the bathroom, leaving laughter and wet drops as a trail.

He followed, his cock leading the way, right to his bedroom, where she had placed herself on hands and knees, legs partially spread, exposed and ready for him.

She tossed him a coy look over her shoulder. "Is this better?"

Since he doubted he could speak coherently at the moment, he simply nodded. With her so temptingly laid out before him, he couldn't stem his impatience. He knelt on the bed behind her and rubbed the head of his cock against her wet lips. He parted them with his swollen head, watching how her pink core trembled as he kept his cock just out of reach.

He pushed just the head in. The very tip.

A shudder went through her.

"More?" he queried. Despite her claims earlier, he didn't want to overwhelm her.

"You talk too much," she grumbled as she thrust backwards. It served to impale him within her sex.

Slick, vise-like heat.

He threw his head back. Feeling the pleasure of being within her. Trying to hold on for just a moment longer but struggling because she felt so gloriously wonderful.

But I can't come without her.

His hips ground against her, slow swirls of pressure, while his finger sought and found her swollen pleasure button.

He rubbed, and thrust, and rubbed, and thrust. And…

She screamed as she came, fisting him tight with her orgasm, drawing forth his own climax with the strength of hers.

He bellowed her name, and he coiled his body around her. He claimed her with his seed and perhaps even his fucking soul.

How could he not? The second time proved maybe even more glorious than the first. Without the impatience of their earlier need, he truly got to savor her. Taste her. Feel her.

She's like a drug. Addictive. He already wanted another hit.

It made him want to sing his feelings aloud. Thing was the song he chose—"Hit Me Baby One More Time" by Britney Spears—made Aria giggle hysterically when he finally gave in and crooned it.

But that laughter only brought them closer. And in his bed that night, they did manage to hit it two times.

Yesssss.

Chapter Nineteen

The noxious smell woke her. She opened her eyes and let out a screech as Princess waggled her butt inches from Aria's nose and let a second fart rip.

"Why you mangy, smelly bitch!" Before she could throttle the little neck with two fingers, Constantine strode into the bedroom.

"What's going on in here? What's all the yelling about?"

"You tell me!" Aria glared at Princess, who sat smugly on the foot of the bed.

"Why are you in such a foul mood?"

"Your dog farted in my face."

His lips quirked. "I highly doubt that."

"I'm telling you she just did."

"How is that even possible? She's sitting on the end of the bed. Besides, Princess is a lady. She doesn't get gassy."

Aria stabbed a finger in the direction of the pooch. "That thing did too fart and on purpose. She doesn't like me."

Constantine scooped his little pooch from the end of the bed, and Aria waited for the chastising to begin.

"Poor Princess. Is that lady being mean to you? And in your own room."

Her jaw dropped.

"Come with Daddy and I'll give you a nice treat."

Pivoting, he went to stroll out the bedroom door.

"Are you fucking kidding me? You're rewarding that thing?"

He turned back and glared. "That *thing* is my dog, and I don't appreciate you insulting her."

With that, he spun around and marched out, and she could have sworn that damned dog wore a smug smirk of satisfaction.

It shouldn't have irked her that Constantine preferred his dog over her. It shouldn't have, but it did. And like fuck was she going to accept it.

Flinging the covers back, she stalked after him.

Stark naked.

"Come back here, angel. I am not done talking to you," she yodeled.

As she entered the kitchen area, he turned around from the front door, which shut with a click.

"Thanks for giving me a chance to get Princess outside and playing along."

She blinked at him as she dumbly said, "What?"

"Princess is having a hard time accepting her daddy has finally brought a mommy into her life."

"Mommy?" The word emerged on a faint squeak.

"We're going to have to be very careful about her feelings while we work on getting her to accept you."

"Hold on." She held up a hand. "You mean that entire 'hey, Aria, woman I fucked like a zillion times last night, is a mean lady, Daddy loves you' was a bullshit cover story to spare your dog's feelings?"

He beamed. "Yes. I'm so glad you understand."

"I don't, but your complete insanity still hasn't deterred me from liking you. A little."

"Don't you mean big?" The smile widened.

"Was it?" She arched a brow. "I don't recall. Maybe you should show me again, angel."

"Any time, my pink-nippled warbler."

Her nose wrinkled even as she laughed. "Okay, that was really not sexy."

"Oh, come on, I thought it was a clever play on words."

She laughed. "No, an awesome play on words is me going woodpecker on you."

His eyes widened. "Okay, you might be right. That sounds totally awesome."

"Then why are you wearing so many clothes?"

Knock. Knock. Knock.

The hard taps at the door stopped Constantine from shoving down his track pants. He frowned. "I wonder why Princess isn't barking."

"Someone you know maybe."

"Princess barks at just about everyone except my nephew. She loves him. Get your sweet ass to the bedroom while I see who it is. Grab the shotgun from the linen closet in the hall, too, would you, just in case."

Shotgun? With the towels and bedding?

Welcome to swamp country.

"What about you? What are you going to use?"

He shot her an incredulous look. "What do you think I'm going to use as intimidation? Me, of course." He let his muscles ripple, and he winked.

She doubted he heard her snort over the next firm knock.

"Go before I give whoever is standing there an eyeful."

"I'm going." But not because she wasn't curious. Constantine did get one thing right. Her buff situation was not exactly conducive for greeting people.

Skipping the shotgun in the hall, because firearms weren't her thing, she hurried to his bedroom and glanced around for something to wear. She could have rummaged through his drawers, yet she found a large T-shirt hanging over a chair. By the looks of it, Constantine had worn it but not deemed it dirty enough yet for the hamper.

She shrugged it on, enjoying the fact it held his scent, all the while listening through the closed door to the soft murmurs of two men. One had to be Constantine, but who was the other?

It must be someone he knows. Although even she had to admit it seemed strange they'd yet to hear a peep out of Princess. The only time the rodent kept quiet was when she stalked and hunted something.

When that dog went on the prowl, she became eerily ghostlike.

Aria had noted the interesting technique when she visited with Cynthia. Princess had a thing for Cynthia's new boyfriend. She enjoyed silently slinking and then lunging with barks and snarls at Daryl's ankle. She never actually bit the man, and yet each time, Daryl screamed, "No blood on the rug."

With the continued silence, she had to wonder, *Is Princess hunting?*

She moved to the window overlooking the backyard. Scanning the area, she didn't see the furball with her pink and rhinestone collar. About to turn away, she noted movement in the foliage at the far end of the yard. She froze and stared as a creature strode from the bayou. A lizard man much like she'd seen before, but she would have sworn the one staring at the house wasn't the same one that had taken Jeffrey. This one stood taller, straighter, with a gaze more piercing, and still human.

I know him.

The flashback hit her hard and fast, and she slumped to Constantine's bed, her mind gripped by the recollection.

She woke in a cage. A freaking cage! The one thing all birds hated.

As Aria jumped to her feet, she noted they were bare and that she still wore her workout clothes—even if she never made it outside after breakfast for a jog. Damned cocoa.

She couldn't help a wrinkle of her nose as the most unpleasant aroma met it. The fabric she wore reeked strongly, the putrid scent of unwashed dog that had rolled in a pile of manure.

But at least she wore clothes, unlike others. Peeking around, she noted other cages, cages with occupants. She couldn't say people. Not quite, even if some still bore human characteristics. But two arms and two legs—and in some cases, human faces—couldn't hide the fur, feathers, and extra limbs some of them sported. It also couldn't mask the madness emanating from them.

What horrific nightmare had she woken to?

Where am I?

A sudden cacophony of sound—grunts, screams, moans, and even a few muttered words—filled the air. "Kill me" and "Kill him" being foremost.

Kill who? The steady thump of feet had her gripping the bars and craning to peek. Someone approached. Someone the other prisoners hated—and feared—with such vehemence.

He soon came into sight. A man, not even an impressive one. The same man who'd loomed over her drugged body.

The bastard who put me in a cage.

He came to a stop in front of her cell. On either side of him, standing as sentinels, monsters.

On the left, she recognized Harold, the dog-like thing that played a part in her abduction and whose stench permeated her clothes and skin.

Someone needs to give him a flea bath and some dental dog cookies for his smell.

The other creature flanking the guy with the fine-stitched loafers appeared humanoid in shape, but that was where all resemblance to humanity ended. Over seven feet, leather-skinned, with giant bat-like wings, he stood with a stoic countenance. His alien features, consisting of a flattened nose, sharp cheekbones, and a ridge atop his head, made his appearance frightening, but it was made more so by his still human eyes.

The man in the loafers chuckled, but she didn't find it reassuring. "I see you're admiring Ace. At least that's what I call him. My ace in the hole when it comes to getting shit done. And our first true success story. Ace used to be a patient here."

"Patient or prisoner?" she retorted.

"The distinction is irrelevant at this point. Ace is one of our greatest accomplishments. A meld of species in order to create the perfect hybrid."

Perfection must lie in the eye of the beholder.

She pointed at Harold. "So if Ace is a success, what do you call that one?"

The smile did not diminish. "Are you talking of Harold? Yes, he didn't quite turn out as expected, and yet, he has his qualities, hence why I keep him. Every genius should have a loyal pet."

"You're a sick bastard."

"Name calling? How rude. Then again, we never were formally introduced. I'm Merrill, the head of this project."

"Project? This is a crime. An abomination."

"Only some of our results can be called that. I will admit, since we started live trials, we've had a few cases that have gone wrong. We keep them here for study. Science learns from its mistakes."

"I've heard rumors of your mistakes making it out in public. They're killing machines."

"Indeed they are, which is why, every so often, we have to let them out or they go quite crazy. The darned things are *always hungry, and sometimes only freshly hunted meat will do. I find them useful for taking care of people who might otherwise cause problems."*

"This is insane."

"You just don't understand progress. You'll thank me after we improve you."

She recoiled, shaking her head. "Don't you dare even think of it. I won't stay here and be your guinea pig. You can't keep me here."

"Do you really think I'm going to let you leave?" Merrill stepped closer to the bars, the better to smirk at her.

"Let me go! You can't keep me here." Panic and fear raised her pulse rate. Her heart fluttered madly in her chest, beating to get free.

"I'm afraid you're not going anywhere, my fine, rare eagle. Not now. Maybe not ever." Merrill's grin widened. "I've got so many uses for a girl with your kind of DNA."

"You can't do this. I work for the SHC. I'm here on their behalf."

"I know. Who do you think warned me you were coming? I've even gotten permission from them to work on you."

"You lie," she claimed. "The SHC would never agree to that. Just like they would never agree to the experiments you've been performing."

"They didn't just agree. They've provided some test subjects. Like you. A nice healthy female in her prime. We're about to start phase two of our project. Interbreeding. Your hips are a little narrower than I would have liked, but C-sections are all the craze nowadays to keep those pussies tight."

The blood in her veins turned to ice as his words

filtered. "You're going to inseminate me?"

"Maybe. Or perhaps we'll try it the old-fashioned way first. Harold would like that, wouldn't you, Harold? I hope you don't mind doggy style. As you can imagine, it's Harold's favorite position."

The lolling tongue on a certain dogman dripped. She might have vomited a little in her mouth.

"You're sick."

"Not anymore. No one has to be. I can cure everyone."

"Making people into monsters isn't a cure."

"Tell that to my bank account."

"I won't let you do this."

"You can't stop me."

During this entire conversation, Ace watched, but said nothing. He said nothing as they brought her for preliminary testing and blood samples. He said nothing when they forced her to call Cynthia and falsely claim everything was peachy keen. Yet, she couldn't entirely hate him. It was because of him she escaped. He'd left the cage unlocked after bringing her back from a session. Not by accident either. She saw him pretend to lock the door to her cell. Saw his pointed stare at her.

She took advantage and ran, ran fast and hard until she ran into a certain snake and his faithful pup.

The thought of them snapped her back to the present. She had to tell Constantine what she remembered. But of more importance at the moment was the fact that Ace had disappeared from the yard. *Where is he now?*

Not knowing meant she should arm herself before joining Constantine. *I should get the gun he mentioned from the linen closet.* Except she didn't have the skill to fire it. The last shotgun she'd tried to shoot had sent her flying a few feet, to land hard on her ass.

She needed a weapon more her size. Something she could hit an opponent with. But what?

She scanned the room and didn't spot a baseball bat or lacrosse stick. Not even a lamp to whack someone with. In that split second while she scanned her options, her gaze landed on the perfect item. She grabbed a sock from the floor and, while in motion, snagged keys and a small trophy of a dog that said, "1st in show." She stuffed the items into the sock and wound the open end in her hand.

As she opened the door of his bedroom, the sounds of a scuffle, along with vicious snarls and barks by Princess, came to her. She paused, gripped by indecision.

What should she do? She could hear the thumps and grunts of a fight. Would one puny sock really make a difference?

Perhaps she should, instead, run for help.

I'm not a coward.

And she wouldn't let him face whatever threat she drew to him by himself. The sock in her hand began to swing.

Stepping into the living room, she stopped dead instead of throwing herself into the fight. Her stillness didn't stop her cotton weapon from moving back and forth like a pendulum.

Shock at the visitors reminded her of

something Merrill had said, that crucial tidbit about the SHC warning him of her arrival. Except only one person had known she was coming.

Parker.

My boss. The guy who sent me here and set me up.

Chapter Twenty

Opening the door, a ready greeting on his lips, Constantine froze as he beheld a stranger. Not too tall, probably just shy of five-foot-ten, the man sported silver hair with only a few hints of darker gray. The fine suit he wore hung on his slender frame.

"Can I help you?" he asked.

Dry lips stretched in a vulpine smile. "Well, if it isn't the snake's son. I'm surprised you stuck around here. As I recall, your father couldn't wait to leave."

At the mention of his father, Constantine froze. "You know my dad?"

"Knew. He worked under me for years. As a matter of fact, he was one of the men I trusted to help start Bittech. Took him months to get all the permits and such sorted. Busy fellow, and I don't just mean on the job site. I'd heard he'd knocked up a local before he returned to our home office."

"You mean my dad never intended to stay?"

"Why would he when he had a perfectly fine family back home?"

Breath whooshed from Constantine, the casual statement a firm emotional punch.

"You lie."

"Why would I? Your father was only in Bitten

Point temporarily. Didn't your mother tell you about the way he vanished every weekend? It was because he returned home every Saturday and Sunday to see his real family." The man smiled. "You have two half-brothers, by the way. They work for me, but lack the skills I prized your father for."

The shocking admission shattered long-held beliefs. *My dad didn't leave because he was afraid of commitment. He left because he already had a family elsewhere.* The truth, while painful and twisted, in a sense set him free.

Dear old dad was a two-timing shit who got my mother pregnant and then walked out on her. But from the sounds of it, while he'd abandoned one family, he did care for another.

If Constantine ignored the bastard, cheating part, it gave him hope that maybe he could have something long-term with Aria. If he survived. Because he didn't need his python's warning hiss to recognize the danger the man before him posed.

"Who are you? And what do you want?" Because holy moly, his oh-shit meter was going crazy. His snake writhed in his mind, begging to get out.

Strike first. Squeeze hard.

An extreme reaction, given the older man in front of him, while a wolf in a suit, would prove no match for his mighty coils.

"Is that any way to address an esteemed member of the Shifter High Council?"

"You're a councilor?" Don't scoff at his ignorance. Constantine didn't pay much mind to shifter politics. He lived his life, in his town, and followed the rules.

He should also note not many could recognize the council members, given the only time people dealt with the SHC was if they'd broken some kind of hardcore law. And even then, local justice tended to be swift.

"Indeed I am, which gives me a lot of power, son."

"I'm not your son."

"Ah, but you could have been. Your mother was a little free with her affections back in the day. Alas, I couldn't stay to oversee things, and your father got to her first."

Constantine couldn't stop his fist from flying, but to his shock, the older man grabbed it—and held it!

"Why are you here?" Constantine growled. He pushed against the man who held him, managing movement only because of his weight. A victory short-lived, as the other guy braced his feet and pushed back.

How is he so freakishly strong?

"I am here because you won't stop asking questions and sticking your nose where you shouldn't. I was willing to let your actions slide out of respect for your father, but then you just had to go and help that stupid bird."

This guy knew about Aria? Shit. "Bird? What bird? The only poultry we have in this house is the chicken in the freezer."

A fierce scowl crossed the man's face. "Don't

lie. I know about the woman staying here."

"No idea who you're talking about. There's no one else here."

Tsk. Tsk. The man shook his head, even as a smile stretched his lips. "You should know better than to try and bullshit me. I've got my men watching the house as we speak. They've reported she's in here. And you're going to tell her to come out."

"Like fuck."

"I thought you might say that, which was why I brought some incentive to obey."

Constantine's blood ran cold as a leathery hand appeared above the councilman's head, the knuckles bristling with coarse fur. Hanging from its grip, one shivering little dog.

"Princess." He couldn't help but breathe her name.

Big eyes lifted to meet his, not in defeat but rather embarrassment. He knew his dog well enough to understand she took the sneaking in on her territory, and worse, getting caught, very personally.

Bad move. Now you've pissed my dog off. And the man. And the snake.

But how to escape from this with everyone intact?

If he didn't call for Aria, they would kill his little princess. *I can't allow that.*

He opened his mouth, but before he could speak, his dog acted. From limp and faking defeat to snarling dynamo with gnashing, sharp teeth. His dog wiggled in the grip holding her prisoner, twisting enough that she managed to sink her canines deep into flesh.

The hairy thing—part gorilla, part fucking nightmare—bellowed and flung his arm outward. Princess let go of her prey and came flying—right at Constantine!

I have to catch her.

He stomped his foot down on the councilor's instep then kicked at a knee. The blow didn't connect. However, it forced the guy to release him. Just in time, too.

Lunging to the side, Constantine caught his dog. However, he couldn't stop his momentum, nor did he want to. He charged forward, but his aim wasn't for either danger posed by the wolf or his henchman, but the umbrella stand by the door.

His fingers curled around the wooden stock of the shotgun his ma kept in case of nighttime critters—or, as she liked to call them, tomorrow night's dinner.

As he yanked it from its spot, he took quick aim, raising the stock of the gun to chest level. He had a moment to look in the eyes—the very human, if crazy eyes—of the hybrid. He hesitated, only a fraction of a second, as he braced the gun against his hip.

Not human, his inner snake hissed.

He applied pressure to the trigger.

BOOM!

The millisecond pause gave the beast the time he needed to dive out the door. A shame. The elephant-sized slug would have probably taken him out.

The loud noise certainly made the old guy eye him with more wariness. The sound also served to hide Aria's arrival, swinging…a sock?

Of more interest than her choice in weapon was her expression. The shock on her face proved unmistakable. Her face turned pale, and her jaw dropped. While whispered, Constantine still caught her words, "Parker? You're behind this. You set me up. How could you?"

Even Constantine paused to hear the reply.

"Because you're a nosy pain in my ass who wouldn't stop harping in my ear about the strange shit happening in Bitten Point." The councilor flung his hands in the air. "I know shit is happening because I'm the one behind it."

"But you're part of the council. You're supposed to protect our kind from discovery and becoming lab rats."

"Times change. The world has changed. It's time we changed with it. I'm tired of cowering for weak humans. We are stronger than them. Better. It is we who should walk with our heads held high."

"You're a monster."

"No, you're looking at one of the successes." Parker flexed an arm. "The strength of a bull, literally. But without the bone-headedness. I've also got the stamina." The wink brought the shotgun in Constantine's grip to bear.

"You've got balls to be flirting with my chick in front of me," Constantine growled.

"The biggest balls, son. I've also got the

upper hand. Submit and maybe I won't hurt you. Why, you might even become one of our success stories."

"I won't let you experiment on me."

"Who said you had a choice? Either come with me quietly or die. The choice is yours."

"Neither," Aria exclaimed. The swinging sock went flying, whipping out and hitting Parker with a solid thunk. The older man staggered, a hand pressed to his face, the gush of blood from his broken nose seeping through his fingers.

"Bitch! You'll pay for that. Bruno, attack!" The injured man screamed the word, and through the open door rushed a thick body, arms tucked tight so that it could fit through the frame.

Constantine didn't have time to turn and shoot before the hairy thing hit him. His arms went wide, and Princess, whom he'd not put down on the floor, went for her second flight that day.

Shit.

He had a moment to note Aria catching his dog before he hit the floor with a thump hard enough to rattle the house.

As he braced his hands against the jaw of the beast trying to bite his face off—a truly ugly blend of monster—he saw the streak of Aria's bare legs as she ran past.

Run. Hide. Her best course of action, given he found himself a little preoccupied with staying alive.

"If you can't subdue him, then kill him," Parker ordered as he strode past. "Be sure to bring his body to the lab when you're done. Even if he's dead, I can use his DNA."

The man who'd dared attack Constantine, in his own home, left. Not much he could do about it, given he wrestled with a monster.

The rabid creature had a thing for digging in its claws. Constantine could have handled a few puncture wounds. It was the lethargy that stole his strength that proved his undoing.

Poison? Shit. That brought a new level of danger to this fight. But he did have one advantage. It wasn't his first time getting drugged by venom. As a boy who'd grown up in the bayou, he'd gotten his fair share of bites over the years, which meant his body knew how to resist it.

He also knew how to fake it.

Sometimes, in order to gain the advantage, a man had to pretend a disadvantage, such as closing his eyes and allowing his body to go limp, hoping that wouldn't result in his throat getting torn out because that Parker dude had a need for him.

The stupid beast bought the act. The heavy weight on his chest moved. Claws scrabbled for purchase on his laminate floor, and Constantine found his arm gripped. He fought hard not to react as the creature dragged him across the floor to the front door. Only once the thing heaved him onto the front step did he jump to his feet with a roar.

Okay, more like a hiss as his snake pushed back the remaining lethargy of the poison and tried to burst free.

The sudden attack caught the monster by surprise, allowing Constantine to grab him by the head and drop to the ground hard.

Crack. A broken neck took care of the rabid Bruno, but Constantine knew there were more. He could smell traces of the flying lizard, a guy currently out of sight, but he proved the less pressing problem because it seemed Parker had brought more allies than expected.

Men, human ones he'd wager by the combat gear they wore and the guns they raised, waited outside a black SUV. Another truck with tinted windows sped away, probably carrying the cowardly Parker. A shame because he so wanted to give the dickwad a hug.

We'll find him later and give him a sssqueeze. First, though, Constantine needed to extricate himself from the current dilemma.

A pair of armed humans held guns trained on him while Princess barked and nipped at their impenetrable boots. If only one of them would lean down so his dog could go for the jugular. Instead, they didn't give Princess a fair chance. They kicked her, sending her little canine body flying.

Princess. No. She landed in a thick bush, a bush that didn't move. A bush that did not bark.

I think they killed my dog.

Unacceptable. And punishable.

With a hiss, part of his snake burst free. For the first time in his life, Constantine managed a half shift. He kept his arms, but his head morphed into a diamond shape, his fangs dropped sharp and curved, and from the top of his tailbone exploded a sinuous tail.

Holy fucking cool. But he'd gloat about his super-duper hybrid shape later.

The tip of his tail lashed at the guy who dared hurt his precious princess. Being humans, at the sight of his majestic serpentine self, they panicked and fired wildly. A few of their darts stuck to his flesh, the tips not managing to penetrate his scaled skin. Puny inconveniences.

He unhinged his jaw and darted at the enemy. They screamed. How human. How useless.

They scattered from his mad dash.

Run fassst. Run far. I will still find you. And hug you. It wasn't just his python that wanted to hug bad guys. He wanted to squeeze them, too, until their eyes popped from their head and they breathed their last.

Cold-blooded excitement fueled his chase, but his prey wasn't as frightened or disorganized as he thought. They broke apart and turned, firing at him. He couldn't avoid both sets of missiles. One of the darts hit the more vulnerable flesh under his arm, stinging and injecting a lethargy-inducing drug into his system.

His adrenaline kept him awake, but for how long? *I've too many things to do before I can sleep.* He needed to find and save Aria, and he didn't know how Princess fared. Losing consciousness now would spell not only his doom, but theirs, too.

I must recover. As his legs refused to carry him with a drunken wobble, his body morphed again, his legs splitting the seams of his pants to fuse together in one long tail. He slithered from the men and their guns, his bottom half undulating on the ground.

It was then he heard the bark. *Princess lives!*

Alive, but not for long if the winged lizard monster leaning over his dog had its way. "Ffffuck offfff," he shouted, rolling the sound on his forked tongue. It was enough to draw the attention of the monster.

It faced him with an evil glare, the madness in its eyes chilling. Not the same creature he'd smelled from before, the one with the human stare. This was the murdering one. The one that, without mercy, had torn Jeffrey's face off.

A true killing machine. But Constantine knew cold-blooded. He lived it every day. And he would live for tomorrow.

His tail whipped from behind and around the body of the lizard thing, but he got him only around the waist before the creature pumped its wings and tried to rise from the ground. Constantine's weight acted like an anchor and kept it grounded. While the thing couldn't fly, it did manage to drag, and Constantine could do nothing to stop it, especially since all his body wanted to do involved finding a nice, warm spot so he could sleep.

The many darts now being fired into him from behind injected him with lethargic poison, more than he could handle.

His strength ebbed, and the thing yanked him to the edge of the yard then onto the outskirts of the bayou. It kept tugging him past the muddy shore so that the water sucked at his body, his oh so heavy body.

In the distance, he could hear Princess barking. He heard the thudding footfalls of the humans approaching, ready to claim their prize.

Too much. Too much for him to handle alone.

He let go of the lizard thing. Let go and let himself sink. Sink in the water and slither down into the darkness that embraced him.

Chapter Twenty-one

Things happened so fast. One moment Aria flung the sock at Parker to distract him, and the next Constantine grappled on the floor with a monster while she made a miraculous catch of a flying dog.

Even more astonishing, Princess allowed herself to stay nestled in Aria's arms without trying to tear a chunk off. Common ground made them temporary allies. But their truce didn't change facts. With Parker threatening, and Constantine occupied, they needed to fly. Like now.

Aria barreled out the door, Princess tucked under her arm. A part of her cringed that she didn't stay to help Constantine, but Aria knew she couldn't stand against Parker. It wasn't just the henhouse that feared wolves.

Outside proved no safer, though. Men with guns aimed her way, and Ace stood blocking her path.

"Move!" she shouted.

Except her orders couldn't compete with Parker's shouted, "Grab the girl and put her in my car."

No. Ace only mouthed the word, but Parker must have seen it because a moment later, Ace hit the ground on his knees, his face a rictus of pain. As Ace curled his fingers around the collar, the burning stench of his flesh made her tummy churn.

Though under obvious torture, he struggled to get to his feet. To obey his master Parker or to help her? She couldn't know for sure. She couldn't take any chances.

Given Ace knelt in her way, Aria did the only thing she could think of. She ran at him. Princess wiggled in her grip, and as Aria leaned down to scoop a handful of rocks, she let the dog loose. Then she rose again, hands full of debris that she flung at his face.

Despite his obvious pain, Ace saw the dirt coming and turned his head, thus missing her as she bowled into him. For a second, as their skin made contact, it sizzled—in a fried chicken kind of way.

Ouch! Hissing in pain, she pushed away from Ace, but not before booting him in the ribs and kicking him in the head to the excited yips of Princess, who darted in with snapping teeth.

One problem out of the way, she kept moving. As she ran, she noted Princess galloped beside her on stubby legs. Something fluttered in her mouth.

Speaking of flutter, a wild beating pounded in her chest.

Free. Fly free. Let me out.

This time the knowledge of her inner eagle didn't frighten or freak her out. Instead, she welcomed the known presence of her friend and invited her in.

Take us to the skies.

Except she couldn't bring forth her bird. She

tried. She pulled. It remained out of reach.

I'm a prisoner! She shared her eagle's horror, yet it wasn't the knowledge that she couldn't shift that made her stumble, but the darts that hit her.

Her tiny frame couldn't handle the injection of so many drugs at once. As she slumped, she heard Parker again. "Grab the girl and bring her. We'll leave the others to clean up the mess."

What mess? The house was clean. Her thoughts whirled in a chaotic circle, her eyes lost focus, but she felt enough to know Ace was the one to scoop her in his arms and toss her in a waiting black truck.

From the backseat, she craned to look, noting as the SUV sped away that the monster that attacked Constantine in the house had dragged his limp body outside.

He's dead. The realization hit her like a hurricane gust, sending her falling, falling, falling into an emotional spiral.

It wasn't the fact that Constantine couldn't help her that traumatized, but more the fact that she'd killed him. She'd brought this danger to his home. And because of her, he was dead.

A chilling realization she didn't get to mull over for long because darkness swallowed her whole, and the next time she woke, she was strapped to a gurney, in a room filled with boxes, packed and ready for shipping.

Where am I? Didn't matter. Wherever she'd found herself didn't bode well.

I'm awake. But for how long? As soon as

Parker or any of the other bastards in this place noticed, they'd drug her again. *Drug me and do unspeakable things.*

But they misjudged if they thought their sleep-inducing darts would stop her for long. She'd experimented a lot growing up, drugs of all kinds. She'd batted at butterflies on 'shrooms. Eaten bags and bags of chips while high. She had a bit of a built-in resistance now when it came to illegal substances. It was why she now resorted to tequila. The fiery liquid could be bought cheaper and was less likely to get her arrested.

And if I get out of here, I am buying the biggest bottle I can find and getting properly sloshed.

If she got out. A frantic urge to escape saw her scrabbling at the straps that held her down.

She eased off the table, her feet bare and sticking out from the bottom edge of the plain cotton gown she wore. The latest fashion statement worn by prisoners held by madmen.

Her naked toes curled from the chill in the floor, but that worried her less than the fact that her knees threatened to buckle.

Oh hell no. She couldn't collapse here. Not now. Who knew what would happen to her the next time she passed out.

I don't want to become a monster. Already she felt something different within her. Her eagle was still present, but it couldn't get out. It was stuck within. A temporary glitch in her ability, or a more serious symptom of the last time she'd found herself a prisoner and injected?

She wavered on her two feet as determination pushed back the lingering drugs. Time to take stock of her situation.

Dire.

Kind of obvious, so she took a peek around. The room must have served as one of their examination spots. Counters along two sides. The gurney she'd eschewed for her own unsteady two feet. Nothing remained in the room except for boxes. Someone was packing up their operation and readying to leave. Given she still lived, she'd guess they meant to bring her with them.

Like hell.

Time to blow this joint, this time for good. Putting her ear to the only door in the room, she took a listen. She could hear muffled voices and the odd stray word or phrase—"Hour," "Trucks waiting," "Time for a coffee?"

It was busy out there. Too busy for her to hope to slip out unnoticed.

And she shouldn't leave without a weapon, but what could she use?

No guards had left a loaded gun for her to use. In opening a box labeled medical supplies, she hit the jackpot.

With shaking hands, she filled the syringes she found wrapped in crinkly plastic with the contents of a few bottles, a chemical cocktail that would either induce hallucinogenic butterflies or nightmares. Either worked.

Armed with one in each hand, she couldn't help the rapid flutter of her heart as she heard the scrape of a key in the lock.

They'd come for her. *But they're not taking me.*

She flattened herself against the side of the door. It opened. A guard took a step in and uttered, "What the fuck?" as he noted the empty gurney.

His surprise proved her advantage.

A mere human mercenary dressed in black fatigues, he couldn't move fast enough to avoid the pair of needles she jabbed him with. She managed to depress the plungers before he flung her away.

She hit the wall with a thud, but while it caused her to shake her head, she recovered. The guard, on the other hand, blinked and blinked again as the cocktail coursed through his bloodstream.

With laced fingers, she swung at him. The super fist knocked the guard hard into the wall, where she plowed into him, shoulder first. He slumped to the floor, eyes shut, unconscious. The additional kick to the head—because she recognized Mr. Handsy from her last stay—was for good riddance.

That done, she went to the door and peeked out. The hustle and bustle had died down. A few cautious steps in the hall showed a lack of windows, but several doors. All of them open. All of the rooms empty. Useless. None of them provided an escape.

However, she'd kind of expected that. If she were correct, Parker had brought her back to Bittech, in the hidden subterranean levels.

I escaped from here once before. She just couldn't remember quite how. She did know she wouldn't find any windows to climb out of, which left her only one real choice. The elevator.

From her last stay, she already knew it required a keycard, which she filched from the snoring guard's body. To avoid discovery, she shut the door behind her, engaging the lock.

An invisible clock ticked in her head, urging her to make haste. Any moment, someone might come looking for her.

She dashed to the elevator and slapped the card against the scanner. It took a moment, but the screen turned from a processing flashing red to a green approved. The elevator door slid open, and she couldn't have said who was more shocked, the human wearing a lab coat who peeked up from his tablet, or her.

"You're not an employee. How did you escape confinement? And what do you think you are doing?" he exclaimed.

"Checking myself out," she muttered as she lunged at him. Amazing how many human doctors worked for Parker. While the doctor might not have an animal side to call on, he was still bigger than her. They grappled. Well, mostly she clung to him and tried to stop him from slamming the red alarm button on the wall of the elevator cab.

A rabid fierceness possessed her. She yelled as she wrestled. Grunted. Stomped her bare feet and thrust with her knee until she made contact. Usually, the expression was hit two birds with one stone, but in this case, she hit two balls with one bird knee.

As the man slumped, she shoved him out of

the elevator doors. It was only as the doors shut that she noted she'd dropped her stolen keycard. It mocked her on the floor outside.

Too late to grab it. The elevator sealed itself and moved. She just didn't know where. She flattened herself against the back of the cab, hands clammy with sweat, a tremble to her frame, but her fear only strengthened her determination to fight.

The elevator jolted to a stop, and she braced herself as the door slid open.

She gaped as one of her jailors, the lizard thing known as Ace, filled the opening. Despite the fact that he'd helped her escape before, she couldn't ignore the fact he'd dragged her here on Parker's orders. Running into him now didn't bode well.

"Going sssomewhere?" Ace hissed, his forked tongue adding sibilance to his words.

"Well, your hospitality has been great and all, but I really think I should be heading out."

As he leaned in closer, Ace's wings fluttered, the leathery sound alien to her ears. She knew what wings sounded like when ruffled, the soft whisper of feathers. This noise had none of that soothing quality.

"Ssso sssoon? I think that isss a good idea."

"What?" She couldn't help replying, her eyes wide.

"Run hard and fassst," he advised. Ace wrapped a leathery hand around her arm, and he pulled her from the elevator. "Run and don't look back."

"I'm not a mouse to be hunted," she hotly

complained, tugging at his iron grip.

Ignoring her feeble attempt, Ace dragged her down the hall to the far end where an EXIT sign mocked her with bright red letters.

It was only as they passed a room with its door open that she noted the slumped body of a guard no longer paying attention to the dozens of monitors.

"What did you do to him?"

"Made sssure he wouldn't pay for my actionsss."

Aria gazed at Ace in askance. What game did he play? He'd just captured her and brought her to Bittech on Parker's orders. Then again, Ace didn't have a choice with the collar around his neck. She'd seen what that collar could do with poor rabid dog, Harold. The smell of burning hair never quite went away.

The controlling collar rested around Ace's neck, a heavy reminder he didn't control his choices or actions.

They've caged him.

A horrible thing to do to anyone, enough to drive many to madness, except Ace didn't exhibit the same rabid fury in his eyes as the other monsters she'd met. As a matter of fact, he showed no emotion at all.

Even now, as he tugged her toward that hope-inspiring EXIT sign, he maintained a placid expression. He didn't seem to care about anything, which made his sudden interest in her all the stranger. *Why does he want me to run?*

Perhaps he toyed with her. Some prey liked to play with their food.

I won't be anyone's dinner.

A door along the hallway opened, and a man in a white lab coat exited. He looked up from his clipboard with a frown. "Where are you taking this subject? And why isn't she in a cage on the truck already with the others?"

"Bite me," was Ace's reply. "I don't answer to you."

The answer seemed to satisfy the guy because he made no move to stop Ace as he tugged her past.

The EXIT sign led to another elevator, one she didn't recall ever seeing, with only one button.

The elevator doors slid shut, enclosing them in the tiny cab. Earlier, she'd travelled without qualm, even if she didn't like the small box. Now, with Ace taking up most of the space, she couldn't help but pant as the confined area closed in on her.

The doors reopened to a cavernous room she'd never seen before. Abandoned skids, empty of cargo, littered the space, as did a few empty cages.

"Where are you taking me?" Aria dug in her heels, but that didn't stop Ace's advance. His grip tightened.

"Ssstop fighting me," he hissed. "I'm trying to help you. It is not sssafe for you here."

"Duh. I think the kidnapping and confinement gave it away. Wait until I tell the SHC."

Ace snorted, a blustery sound. "Who do you think is running this place?"

He confirmed what Parker claimed, and her

heart sank. But that didn't mean she didn't pump him for more info. She'd need every bit of evidence she could get if she was going to convince people to do something about the corruption on the council. "Bittech is managed by some dude and his son."

"Who get their orders from sssomeone on the council. And that person wants you out of the way."

"Parker." She growled his name.

"Parker is nothing but a lackey, no matter how big he might think he isss."

Another player involved? Just how high did this travesty go? "Why did he come after me?" Because Parker was the one who'd encouraged her to find out all she could when she expressed an interest in the reports she'd seen.

"Parker goes after everyone who dares come sssnooping."

Snooping? She'd barely even begun asking questions. "People are going to come looking for me, especially if I go missing again."

"At this point, I don't think Parker cares."

"Because he and the rest of the people working for him have gone cuckoo." How else to explain the insanity?

"Parker's unfortunately all too sane, even though he's played with some of the drugs they're developing here. Merrill, on the other hand, is nutsss. Almost as nutsss as the other experiments."

"Are you crazy?"

His steady gaze met and held hers. "I'm a man trapped in a monsssster's body. What do you think?"

She thought he avoided the question. "Where are you taking me?" If he said the kitchen for a dash of salt and pepper, she'd know the answer.

"You have to leave now before it'sss too late. Eventsss are about to escalate. People are going to get hurt."

Matching her short pace to his longer one, Aria frowned as she asked, "Why are you helping me? Why do you care?"

An ugly chuckle rumbled from him. "I don't care. But anything that fucksss with Parker and his sssycophants works for me."

"Why do you stay if you hate them so much?"

At the end of the hall, Ace paused before a closed door without any markings. "Because where would I go? Monsssters don't get to live in the real world."

The door they went through didn't require a keycard. The push bar creaked as Ace shoved it. On the other side, there was no elevator to use, just a long set of stairs that stretched upward. She eyed them with a groan.

"Is this the only way out?"

"The only way you stand a chance. If I take you out the main entrance, you'll never make it out of here alive. Your bessst bet isss to get lossst in the swamp."

The swamp? Again. "Why does that sound familiar?"

"Because that'sss how I helped you essscape

lassst time. But then, instead of leaving town, you ssstuck around."

Not her fault she'd lost her memory. She had time to mentally grumble about the prospect of once more crossing the swamp as she trudged up the stairs.

At the top, she huffed a little as Ace waited for her by the door.

Despite his admission, she couldn't help a nervous query. "How do I know you're not setting me up?"

Human eyes in a reptile face glanced at her. "You don't. You want to ssstay inssside, then ssstay." He released her arm and moved away as the door swung open at his shove. "But, if you ssstay, you'll ending up wishing you'd died."

With those final words, Ace turned on his heel and took the stairs down, two by two, the pointed ridge of his wings jutting above his shoulders. She spent a moment staring and realizing, despite his alien appearance, Ace remained a guy, a guy stuck between a rock and an even harder place. He was right. Where could he go that people wouldn't hunt him?

She turned her gaze toward the open door, where the pungent scent of the bayou called.

Freedom? It seemed too easy. She took a step then another, emerging from the hatch into a hillock, camouflaged from all but the closest inspection.

No strident alarms blared. She took a few more steps, clearing the doorway completely, and felt the cool pre-dusk air on her face.

It seemed she'd spent more time than expected in her cell. The colorful rays of a setting sun painted the horizon. A beam of sunlight crested the treetops, and its warm rays bathed her skin. Much like a blossom, she absorbed it, inhaled deeply of the life and vitality flowing all around her in the swamp.

Stop smelling the freaking flowers and get your ass moving.

A helping hand on getting out by Ace didn't mean she should waste time. Who knew when Parker or Merrill would notice she'd gone? Once they did, the hunt would happen. She knew too much.

A tug on the door and the hydraulics kicked in, sucking the portal into its slot and sealing it shut. The greenery and rock stuck to the surface, and once closed, it blended in.

She wouldn't be going back that way, which meant no going back now. Turning, she surveyed the area.

It seemed she stood on a bit of an island. Nothing really big enough to even mark on a map, but large enough for this secret exit and a ramshackle dock. While the dock boards rotted, the dock still served a purpose as a landing point for the two boats tied there. This deep in the swamp, it was the best way for landlubbers to move around.

Given the swamp was her escape, she didn't want to make it easy for Merrill and his disreputable gang to follow. She quickly unlashed the blue boat, tossing the loose mooring rope into it before giving it a shove. Then she worked on the knot holding the other craft, a camouflage-colored, flat-bottomed fishing craft with a small motor at the back. Just as she tugged the last knot loose, it started.

A siren whirred to life, not loud or outside, but from within the compound itself. Its strident blast made the ground on the hillock hum, and that, in turn, vibrated the dock. Even the water nearby shivered.

It lasted less than a minute before stopping.

Odd. She took it as a sign she should get going.

Before she could step into the bobbing craft, the door in the hill cranked open and Merrill stepped out with a smarmy expression and an overtly cheerful, "Leaving so soon?"

Chapter Twenty-two

Once the drugs dissipated from his system, Constantine rose from the water, a sea serpent cresting the surface, pissed but alive. For some reason, people seemed to forget that his snake thrived in aquatic conditions. While a python couldn't truly breathe underwater like a fish, he could, however, remained submerged for up to thirty minutes. All the time he needed to let the poison leach from his system and for the assholes who'd attacked him to take off.

How shoddy of his enemy to leave thinking he was dead. Not dead. Not happy. And not going to let them keep his woman. He also wanted vengeance for his dog.

You abandoned Aria and Princess.

The realization burned, then again, had he died in a futile battle, they'd have no one to come to their rescue.

As Constantine slogged from the swamp, his anger burned even hotter as he noted the destruction of his home. The rabid lizard seemed unhappy at the loss of its prey. Not a single window remained intact. The siding lay strewn across the lawn in a ripped and senseless mess. All the work he'd put into the place, all the money, all the love, destroyed because of a power-hungry bastard and his sick pets.

Speaking of pet, a sharp yip drew his gaze down, and he could have wept—manly tears of course—when he noted his little dog loping at him sideways, tongue lolling.

"Princess!" He swept her into his arms and couldn't help but laugh as she lapped his face in excitement. "I'm so glad you're safe."

Yip. Translation: *I am going to pee myself I'm so happy you're back.*

"I don't suppose Aria got away?"

Gruff.

"No, eh?" His lips turned down. "That blows because you know I can't let them keep her. I have to go find her. But how and where?"

In his arms, Princess wiggled, her signal she wanted to be let down. He placed her on the grass and watched her dive toward a bush. She emerged with something in her mouth. She dropped it at his feet and sat, tail quivering, ears perked.

He knelt and whistled. "I'll be damned, Princess. Where did you get a keycard for Bittech from?" Who cared? His dog might have given him the solution to rescuing his woman.

A smart man, the first thing Constantine meant to do before haring off to save his girl was to call for backup. Except his phone lay smashed on the ground, and his ma had long ago gotten rid of their house phone since they both had cells. This meant he had no other means of outside communication.

Fuck.

He could drive to find help, but every minute he wasted was a minute Aria spent in their grasp. Still, storming Bittech on his own was nuts. He'd have to make at least one detour to get the ball of attack rolling. He snagged his keys and headed out to his truck.

It shouldn't have surprised him they'd trashed his vehicle, but it did hurt. He loved that gas-guzzling beast.

Another person might have given up at this point. Not Constantine. There was more than one way to get around the bayou.

"Wanna go for a swamp cruise?" he asked Princess as he stripped.

Yip-yip.

Some people might have found it odd to see a giant snake, slithering through the watery marsh, a canvas sack clutched in its teeth but, strangest of all, would have been the little dog, standing atop the head, keeping her paws dry.

Mock him or his dog and he would hug you to death.

The afternoon waned as he moved, time passing more quickly than he liked given he'd had to take a watery route.

Arriving near the Bittech property, he slithered from the water with Princess leaping off once they hit solid and dry ground.

The change from snake to man took but a moment, the wet wipes in his waterproof sack cleaning most of the bayou from his skin and the clothes he pulled out dry and loose in case he needed to shed them in a hurry.

Somehow, he didn't think slithering into Bittech or striding in naked and covered in mud would get him where he needed to go. The card Princess stole, he tucked into his pants pocket.

With long strides, he approached the building, Princess trotting at his heels. The parking lot was almost empty except for a large moving truck that rumbled as the engine idled.

As he approached, someone slammed down the roll-top door at the rear of it. In moments, the driver, a guy he didn't recognize in a ball cap and visored glasses, got into the vehicle. It rolled off with a groan of a big engine and a puff of diesel smoke.

Ignoring the vehicle, Constantine approached the main building. The sun dipping deep in the west meant this side of the lot found itself bathed in shadow, yet he still saw a form detach itself from the building, the bright red tip of a cigarette marking its trajectory as it fell to the ground.

"Constantine, what the hell are you doing here?" Wes asked as he got closer.

"I'm here for Aria."

"Your girl's not here."

She's here. His snake sense said so. He peeked through the glass doors to the lobby and noted it seemed stripped bare. Even the potted plants were gone.

"What's going on? What was that truck doing here? And where is all the shit you used to have in the lobby?"

"Gone. Sudden orders from above. Some

kind of inspection said the building was unsafe. Sinking into the bayou apparently. So they're moving the operation."

A convenient excuse that Constantine didn't let slide. "Moving or going into hiding?"

Wes frowned. "What makes you say that?"

"Because the guys who attacked me at my house today were from here. And, if that's the case, it makes me wonder if you've been bullshitting us all along."

Wes tapped a cigarette out of his pack and slid it between his lips, but didn't light it. "Bullshitting you how? I'm the one who has been saying for a while there's something shitty happening here."

"And yet, you haven't found a clue."

"Because there's nothing to find." Wes swept an arm behind him at the building. "What you see is what you get."

"Is it?"

"Are you calling me a liar? Don't believe me? Then be my guest. The place is wide open, buddy. Go and search it. You'll see your lady friend isn't there."

"Aren't you going to come with me?"

"Need me to hold your hand?"

Honk. The horn prevented Constantine from answering.

Wes turned as a car rounded the building and flashed its lights. "Fuck. I gotta go. That's my boss trying to get my attention."

"I'm going in there," Constantine warned.

"Knock yourself out. You won't find anything on those floors."

I know. He recalled what Aria had said after one of her flashbacks. At the time, he'd scoffed, but now, fingering the keycard in his pocket, he wondered.

They're hiding a whole secret lab under the building, she'd insisted.

A secret lab that didn't seem so farfetched since their discovery of old tunnels used by Merrill and his pet dog to move around without notice.

Upon entering the building, he noted no one was there to pay him any mind. The strip-down operation became truly apparent with only items that were truly bolted down being left behind. Even the chairs in the reception area had vanished.

As Constantine entered the elevator, he peeked at the buttons and found himself stymied by his lack of choices. B, 1, 2, 3. "It would really help if they labeled the dungeon lair," he grumbled to Princess, who sat at his feet.

Despite the handy buttons, Constantine had to wonder if the elevator went anywhere else. He jabbed at the B button. The elevator went down and opened onto a utility area loud with the hum of machinery. He pressed all the buttons one by one. Then together.

He kept seeing the same floors over and over, but not a sign or scent of Aria. Nothing to make him believe there was anything else to Bittech.

Frustrated, he exited into the lobby. Now what?

He exited the building and went around it, noting as he moved, the sun truly dipping. Twilight would soon arrive, making his search even harder.

If I'm even in the right place. The keycard in his pocket seemed to say so.

Hold on a second. He pulled the card from his pocket with the sudden realization he'd not used it once while inside. Of course, all the doors were open, wide open on empty rooms. Still, though, he didn't recall seeing a place to use it.

That in and of itself niggled his suspicious side.

Moving around the building, he arrived at the back. The loading dock area proved empty but for one lone truck. A big, white cube truck with no driver.

Strange, but that wasn't what caught his attention. Upon going around to the back of the vehicle, he sniffed.

I smell an alien.

Let's go give it a hug.

Chapter Twenty-three

"Fuck." Vulgar, yet very apt Aria thought as the mad lizard with the bat wings came darting through the hidden door first, his hiss of excitement unmistakable.

After it came a canine creature much like Harold, who scuttled on all fours.

Behind them both strolled Merrill, hand outstretched, a little black remote in it. Of more concern was Ace, who staggered behind and held a tranquilizer gun.

She almost opened her mouth to accuse him of setting her up, except she noted Ace had the fingers of his free hand on his collar. His expression seemed tauter than usual. Even though she stood a few yards away, she smelled burning flesh.

Whatever Ace did now, it wasn't willingly.

I need to fly. She pulled at her inner eagle, willing it to come forth. But as before, her eagle refused to listen.

And Merrill laughed. "What's wrong? Are your wings not working?"

"What did you do to me?"

"Something I do to all new test subjects. Inhibit your ability to change. A neat trick, wouldn't you say?"

No, because it brought forth a fluttery panic

and she couldn't help but ask, "How long does it last?"

"Only a few days. I've yet to have my scientists perfect the formula. But never fear, it will last long enough to get you to our new installation where a shiny new cell awaits, along with your next dosage."

She took a step back. "You won't get away with what you're doing. Too many people know about Bittech and the experiments."

"I know. A shame. Packing up and moving is such a pain in the ass. But Parker's promised me an even better location, one where I'll have access to even more shifter genomes. Now be a good girl and come with me."

"Never."

"Ooh, a bad girl. No wonder Harold wanted you so much. A shame he slipped his leash and got impatient. But never fear, my faithful sidekick, Fang here will be more than happy to help me with my next round of experiments. My pet lizard, though, can only watch. He has a tendency of ripping apart his paramours. And you're too precious to lose quite yet."

Ice filled her veins. "I won't let you do this."

"You won't have a choice." Merrill smiled as he said, "Anytime now, Ace."

Ace looked down at the gun, but didn't move otherwise.

Merrill's gloating expression turned sour, and she noted his finger holding down a button on the remote. "I said shoot her, you stupid fucking lizard."

"No." The single syllable was pushed out by the man with leathery skin. The whiff of roasting flesh tickled her nose.

In that moment, she felt sorry for him, and thankful. Despite the pain, he was trying to help her, and what was she doing? Standing around like a fucking idiot.

"Shoot her, goddammit." Merrill blew spittle with his angry command.

"Fuck you."

Not liking that answer, Merrill did something with his remote that drew a sharp gasp from Ace.

Body gripped in a convulsion, Ace couldn't hold on to the gun. Hell, he couldn't even remain upright. He hit the ground twitching.

Leaving Aria truly alone with a madman and his pets. His very, very dangerous pets.

"Grab her, but don't damage her. We need her whole for what I have planned."

"As my massster commandsss."

Grawr.

"Like hell," she retorted. The camouflage boat she'd untied had drifted a few feet from the dock. It didn't take much of a leap to land in it. She thanked her lightweight, petite frame for it not tipping over. Although it was close. She waved her arms for balance as she adjusted to the sway and made her way to the engine.

She plopped onto the last seat on the boat as Fang came tearing at the dock on all fours, his barely human eyes wild with animal hunger.

She couldn't look at him and start the motor

at the same time. Besides, who wanted to look insanity and death in the eye?

A quick glance down and she noted the pull cord. Yank. *Whirrrr.* Yank harder. *Whirr.* A third and the motor turned over. *Rrrr. Rrr.* She slapped the throttle.

Vroom.

The boat shot forward and just in time. There was a splash in the wake she'd just left as Fang leaped after her.

Hysteria at the situation made her wonder just how bad he'd reek of wet dog when he got out.

On the shore, Merrill stood waving his remote, his face a mottled red. "She's getting away. Fly after her, you overgrown fucking lizard."

The mad one flapped his leathery wings and lifted from shore.

As the boat gathered momentum, drawing her farther from the hillock, she couldn't help a hysterical laugh and even waved bye-bye to Merrill.

She'd escaped. Fang and his dog paddle would never catch her. Merrill was stuck on shore. And if she could make it to the tree line only yards away, even his flying pet wouldn't be able to catch her.

I'm free. Free to tell everyone in the shifter world what happened beneath the floors of Bittech Institute.

A reckoning would come once she told the shifter world. Merrill and Parker might take off before the hammer came down, but no matter. They could run and hide, but those seeking justice would find them.

And I will help in the hunt. They would pay for what they'd done.

A sudden engine noise had her craning, and she noted that a new man must have emerged from the open door on the hillock. The guard and Fang piled into the boat she'd set adrift. Damn Fang for grabbing it and dragging it back. Stupid dog knew how to fetch.

But she did have a head start and less weight in her vessel. What did chill her to the bones, though, was the shrill cry in the sky. The crazy lizard hunted.

Maybe he'll get distracted by something in the swamp.

A vain wish.

A shadow swept over her. She didn't need to peek upwards to guess what it was. She veered her boat under the concealing fronds of the boughs on a drooping tree and ducked low as she puttered through them, sharply turning a few times. As she guided her craft through almost hidden intersections, she fervently prayed she'd not only lose her tail, but also the eyes in the sky.

When she felt she'd gone far enough, she killed the motor and let it drift as she listened.

The hum of insects filled the air, along with the gentle sucking sound of water lapping at a muddy shore.

Then she heard it, the piercing ululation of a hunter overhead. Had it spotted her? She craned to look above. However, the heavy foliage screened her view. So where was the hunter?

She kept low with her hand on the pull cord of the motor, yet when a creature finally revealed itself, it surged from under her boat, tipping her into the water!

Chapter Twenty-four

The discovery of the scent revived him.

Finally a clue. Loping to the back of the truck, he grabbed the lip of the roll down and pushed. It went ratcheting upward, a noisy indication of his presence, which hid his gasp.

Within the truck he found boxes, stacked on top of each other, and a cage. A big, empty cage.

Princess yipped, drawing his attention. Turning, he noticed she seemed very interested in the utility shed at the back end of the loading dock parking area. A pretty big shed, actually, for the amount and size of yard tools this place needed. As he neared it, he realized the shed also hummed.

Perhaps Bittech kept a backup generator outside. Not unheard of, but of more interest was his dog. Parked in front of the closed access door sat Princess. She cocked her head and then pawed at the door.

The realization it required a keycard to open galvanized him. Throughout his search of Bittech, not once had he used the card in his pocket. He'd not needed to because that Bittech was just a front.

Sliding the plastic rectangle free, he popped it into the card slot. The light went from red to green. *Click.*

He pulled the door open and stepped into an

empty room. The entire shed was swept clean, not a single lawn tool to be seen. But at the back, dull metal door gleaming, one elevator door—with a card slot.

"What do you think, Princess? Is this the secret lair?"

Yip.

The card once again gave him access. The doors slid open, and he stepped in, the myriad of smells setting off a chain reaction of recognition and repugnance. Alien, lizard, simian… All the flavors were there, along with human. And was it wishful thinking, or did he detect a hint of Aria's sweet scent?

The walls of the elevator didn't prove exciting. Scuffed metal panels with a rail running along the back. No buttons here. Just a screen saying, *Please scan your access card.*

He flashed it and heard a beep. The screen changed and showed several choices. Instead of numbers, the floors possessed names: *Admin, Research, Holding.*

The first option sounded as if it might have folks who would probably recognize he didn't belong. Research would probably involve guys in white coats, if there were any left. It didn't take a genius to realize Parker and his merry band were jumping ship.

Option number three it is. Call it a hunch, but he'd wager that was where they kept their prisoners.

The smooth gait of the elevator didn't let him know how far he sank, but it felt as if he descended a while. It made him wonder how the hell they'd built such a place and without anyone noticing. Then again, shifters were kings when it came to hiding.

As the elevator descended, anticipation churned in his gut. His fists clenched at his sides. What would he find? Aria was so delicate. It wouldn't take much to hurt her. Or was she already gone? Taken away in one of those trucks.

No. He refused to believe he'd arrived too late. The belief didn't dispel the anxiety, which, he might add, didn't mean he was afraid or about to turn yellow-bellied.

Nothing wrong with caring. And if you didn't agree, he'd happily take you out to the swamp for a big hug until you changed your mind.

The doors slid open with only the slightest *whoosh*. Braced, he waited for someone or something to jump at him. But there was nothing to see, just an abandoned counter with a swivel chair on castors and the dusty rectangle left behind to show where a monitor used to sit.

Constantine walked the long hall lined with cages. Empty cages. Mostly. A few held misshapen lumps that emitted a foul stench. Others had blankets strewn in them. One cell even held an abandoned stuffed bear.

The scents stung his nose, the scent of wrongness. Alien. Fear…

At the bars of one cage, he stopped. Sniffed.

Aria was here. This was her cage. The one he'd wager she escaped from before finding him. He spun around, horrified at what it all meant.

His dog whined, and he turned to find her standing before a cage. He ran to her, wondering if she'd found a clue, only to skid to a stop.

It seemed they'd not taken everyone. In the cage, something wrapped in a woolen blanket moved. A head lifted, the face covered by dank and stringy hair.

"Help me," it whispered.

Constantine gripped the bars. "Do you know where they hide the key?"

"Help me." The figure scuttled closer to the cage, remaining on all fours. Princess backed away, a low growl rumbling.

The alien aroma left a bad tang in his nose, but Constantine didn't flee. It wasn't its—or was that a her?—fault she'd become something less human. Something twisted.

He crouched down as she came close to the bars. "How can I help you?"

With a whip of her head, the hair flew back, and mandibles snapped at his gripping fingers. Constantine fell backwards, digits intact, but one of them oozing blood as the tip of her pincer mouth caught him.

The blanket fell away, and he could now see the true horror within the cage. Less woman, more spider, with stunted legs growing from her torso covered in bristled hair. Most horrifying, she maintained some human features, and a voice.

"Help me. Meat. Feed me. Meat. Hungry." She cackled.

He shivered.

The pointed tips of her legs, covered in human flesh, jabbed through the bars, but Constantine, taking a moment to scoop his dog first, was already fleeing. They could take his fucking man card for running. No way was he sticking around this place. Not when Aria wasn't here. He had to find her before they turned the woman he thought of as his into one of those things.

With his dog tucked under his arm, he returned to the elevator and hit the level above. There he found more signs of a rapid departure in the shape of doors left open, a few boxes fallen and a general air of rapid abandonment.

And in one room, Aria's scent and a snoring body. Not hers, but that of a guard.

Aria had been here, and recently, too. Now if only he could follow her scent trail. However, the varied and frenetic mishmash of odors from the mass exodus overpowered her more delicate bouquet. A quick search of the other rooms down the hall didn't find any trace of her, so he went up another level.

He exited to find more chaos. More abandoned offices with open drawers, loose papers, dusty marks of items taken.

But as he went down the hall, he caught a scent. Her scent. He ran toward the red EXIT sign at the far end. He pushed through the door to find another elevator. And then a cavernous room and, at the far end, another door and stairs. All along the way, her scent taunted.

He took the stairs in threes, bolting up them, urgency fueling his speed. At the top, he paused only a moment before slamming open the door and startling a man. A man he knew by face and name.

"You're Merrill."

"How did you get here?"

Constantine smiled, the chill smile of a predator who had cornered his prey. "Does it matter? Where's Aria?"

"Gone. Hopefully dead, the problematic bitch."

At those words, Constantine charged him. And once the man lay dead—*regenerate from that, asshole!*—he went looking for his chick.

Chapter Twenty-five

The boat tilted over, and she hit the water with a splash, yet didn't sink. The heavy coils of a sinuous body wrapped around her, but forget panic. She wanted to smile instead.

As her head broke the surface of the water, she sucked in a breath of air, but didn't scream as she came face to face with a python.

"Hello, angel."

A forked tongue flicked, and Constantine hissed.

"I don't think this is the time for tongue." She smirked. "How about later if we make it out alive?"

The serpentine head bobbed in agreement.

A cry shrieked from the sky overhead. Her reptilian lover peeked upward.

"Merrill's pet is looking for me," she explained.

Was it possible for a snake to grin?

Weaving in the water, Constantine carried her, drawing her past the remains of the second boat, Fang and the other occupant nowhere to be seen.

Nessie had nothing on her serpent.

She heard the fierce bark of a certain Princess, and she strained to peek. Only once she saw did she exhort him to, "Hurry before that lizard makes Princess into a snack."

Although, Princess seemed determined to prevail, even against the odds. The valiant dog darted to and fro, avoiding the reaching talons of a flying lizard no longer controlled by a certain remote. Probably on account of Merrill lying on the ground with his head tilted at an unnatural angle.

Before they could hit the shore and rescue her, Princess squealed as the thing scooped her in a clawed hand. It sprang into the air, taking the dog with it.

"Oh, hell no. If anyone gets to eat that thing, it's me," she grumbled. Her feet hit the ground, her wet gown came off, and she strained. Hard as she could. She pulled on the essence of her eagle. Pulled and pulled and...

A caw of success vibrated on her lips as her flesh turned to feathers, arms extended into wings. Pushing with her legs, she sprang into the air and extended her wings. A few mighty flaps and she was airborne. She immediately followed the lizard bastard.

She uttered a challenging cry. It was answered, the lizard thing halting in mid-air and hovering. The creature held Princess aloft, grinned, and then opened its mouth wide.

Intending to eat the dog didn't mean it managed to. Princess turned rabid, twisting her head far enough that she managed to chomp it on the wrist. The leathery skin might be tough, but it proved no match for needle-like, determined teeth.

A screech from the creature and it forgot its plan to eat the furry snack. Of course, Princess's new situation, which involved plummeting to the ground, wasn't any better.

A choice faced Aria; let her mighty eagle take down the enemy in the sky or save one stupid little, annoying dog.

The things I do for the man I care about.

She plummeted, her wings tucked tight to her body. Streamlined, she arrowed through the sky, hurtling after the little furry form. As she neared the point of no return in her dive, she reached out. The hook of her claw caught on the collar Princess wore, and she banked out of her suicide plunge, catching the air currents before they crashed into the ground.

Of the lizard monster, there was no sign. He'd escaped.

For now.

As she hit the ground, she changed until she wore her own body. A body that got crushed against another naked one as a happy Constantine hugged her.

"I'm so glad you're safe."

"Are you talking about me or your dog?" she asked against his bare chest, Princess's furry body squished between them.

"Do I have to answer?"

She snorted. "Probably best if you don't."

Yip. Princess agreed.

As he released her, she took a peek around. "I see you took care of Merrill, but what happened to Ace?"

"Who?"

"The other lizard guy. The one who helped me escape. He was here when I took off in the boat."

Constantine shrugged. "No idea. When I came out on the hill, only Merrill was here. Dumb fuck thought he was tough."

"Proved him wrong?"

"I proved a hug is mightier than the fist." He grinned.

The ground under foot rumbled, enough that she reached out to steady herself using his rock-hard chest. A thick arm curled around her waist.

"What was that?" she asked.

Smoke billowed from the door leading back into the secret installation.

"I think someone just cleaned up some loose ends."

"So how do we get out of here?"

As he glanced at the swamp, she groaned. "Oh, hell no. I am not going back in there."

Luckily, she didn't have to. Her eagle was now hers to call upon again.

With night blanketing Bitten Point, hopefully no one noticed the eagle skimming the swamp, keeping a close watch on a snake, who wore a little dog as a hat.

Landing in the yard behind his house, she shifted back and gasped. "Constantine. Your poor house." She took in the damage and couldn't help the guilt that filled her.

"I don't give a fuck about the house. You and

Princess are safe. That's what matters."

As was his mother and brother and sister-in-law and their kid and a whole bunch of other people who poured into the yard from the house all demanding answers and, after some red-cheeked moments, offering them some robes.

The most astonishing part of that evening in the yard wasn't the fact that they lit a firepit and roasted hot dogs and marshmallows over it, or the fact that no one thought it odd Constantine held her perched in his lap with Princess in hers. The weirdest part was how they all acted as if she belonged.

Here. With him.

And the urge to fly, to seek new skies, to drift upon new winds, didn't strike.

Can I make a life here, with him? What of the better question, did Constantine want her to stay?

Chapter Twenty-six

It seemed to take forever before everyone left. A man loved that his friends and family cared, but dammit, right now Constantine cared about more important things, such as peeling that robe from Aria, bathing every inch of her body, and then checking her to make sure for himself that she had emerged unscathed from her ordeal.

The house with its wreckage couldn't handle them for the night, so Caleb loaned him some money and dropped him and Aria off at a motel—run by shifters, so no questions were asked about their lack of normal clothing.

Once the motel room door closed, Constantine turned to Aria with a smile. "At last. I've got you alone."

Yip.

Aria snickered. "Better explain that to your dog."

But Princess didn't require explanation. With a look of disgust, his dog jumped onto an armchair and curled into a ball.

Poor jealous baby. She'd come around. He hoped.

"Shower time," he announced.

She arched a brow. "Is that just your way of getting me naked again?"

"Yes."

"Why didn't you just say so?" She laughed, but she also dropped the robe to the floor and led the way into the white-tile washroom. The brat even bent over to turn on the tap.

It was enough to strangle a man.

Hug her.

Good idea. He wrapped her in his arms, hugging her tight to him, closing his eyes as he finally relaxed enough to realize she was safe.

"You're squishing me," she said when she finally realized he wasn't letting go.

"Get used to it," he retorted while manhandling her so she had to face him.

"You like hugging, don't you?"

He couldn't help but smile. "Just a bit."

"I'm good with that." Her arms wound around him and squeezed just as tightly.

Perfection. However, their bodies that closely entwined meant he didn't get to look at her. And he really, *really*, wanted to take a peek.

Lifting her, he climbed into the shower. Only then did he release his grip on her.

With a seductive smile, she leaned back against the tile wall. "So in all the excitement, I don't know if I said thank you for coming to rescue me."

His eyes tracked the finger that drew a line between her breasts and then dipped lower. "If you ask me, you were doing a pretty damned good job of saving yourself."

"Guess I did, but a girl does like to know she can rely on her man." She paused, and she peeked at him, a coy smile curving her lips. "And I think this girl should thank the angel who saved her."

"No need to thank. I'd do anything for you." Never had he spoken truer.

"Really? You'd do anything? Then wash me, would you, because I am so done with smelling like a swamp." She wrinkled her nose, and he laughed.

"Your wish is my command."

The soap sat on the dish inset within the tile wall. He made quick work of its wrapper. The lemon scent filled the shower as he lathered his hands. He rubbed those soapy palms over her breasts, cupping them and watching with hunger as those berries puckered, begging for a bite. He saw no reason to wait. He lowered his face and brushed it across an erect nub, lapped, spat, and rinsed his mouth.

"Too clean?" she teased.

"You're evil to tease a man suffering," he mumbled.

"What are you going to do about it?"

Why tease her right back, of course.

She inhaled sharply as he dipped in for another taste. A bite. Her back arched, and she thrust her breasts at him, begging him to do more than flick his tongue. He ignored her invitation and spent more time circling around the erect tip.

Lithe fingers weaved through his hair, tugging him close, attempting to force his mouth to take her engorged nipple. As if she had the strength to make him do anything.

He chuckled, blowing hotly on her nipples, loving how they tightened further.

"Bite them," she begged.

"Giving me orders?" Hot, but not what he had planned. He stood, forcing her hands to release their grip. Before they could choose a new spot, he clasped them in an iron fist and pushed them over Aria's head.

She arched, thrusting her body at him, the warm water sluicing down her frame.

With his free hand, he gathered the bar of soap. "I don't believe I was done with this." With the slippery soap in hand, he pressed against her mound, rubbing against her downy curls. A shudder went through her.

He could understand how she felt. His whole body hummed, vibrated as if full of electricity. A live wire waiting to zap.

His soapy hand slid between her parted thighs, brushing over the petals of her sex. Her breath caught, and her body went taut, anticipation heavy between them.

With her hands still braced over her head, he kept rubbing against her core while dipping his head for another taste of those nipples.

She cried out. She thrashed. But sweetest of all, she moaned.

Need burned within him. Arousal made him painfully erect.

"I don't think I can wait any longer."

"Then don't," she replied.

Releasing her hands, he palmed her waist and hoisted her, high enough that her legs came around his waist. Her arms wrapped loosely around his neck. He peered between their bodies, admiring the slickness of their skin. The tip of him brushed against her wet curls. By angling his hips, the head of his cock pressed against her sex.

She sucked in a breath as he pushed in, watching his shaft slide into her slick heat. Deeper. Deeper. Fully seated.

And her channel constricted him and hugged him so deliciously tight.

With a gasp of pleasure, he pulled out then slammed back in. Out. In. Her legs squeezed around his shanks, holding him close, burying him within her welcome heat.

He couldn't help but drop his head so that his forehead pressed against hers. The soft pants of her breaths fluttered over his skin as he seesawed in and out of her.

The sharp nails in his shoulders were but a pinch and meant she'd reached her cusp. He thrust deeply, one last time, so deep inside her, then threw his head back and hissed.

Hissed as her channel hugged him tight.

Sucked in a ragged breath as her sex undulated around him.

Held her close knowing he would never, ever let her go.

Oursss.

Epilogue

Snuggled against him later in the motel bed, Aria couldn't help but think that, despite everything that had happened, she'd never been more happy or felt more at home.

She sighed with contentment, so utterly blissful...until the dog stuck her cold, wet nose against her spine.

With a scream, she sat upright. "Your dog hates me."

"Love me, love my dog." Rolling onto his back, hands laced behind his head, Constantine smirked.

She glared at Princess. Princess glared back. And then she saw it, the twinkle of mischief in the dog's eye. The slight curl of a lip.

"Your dog is sly."

"Yup."

"Ferocious."

"Yup."

"Kind of cute if you don't mind the fact she could tear out the tendons in your ankle."

"See, I knew she'd grow on you."

"Don't think this means I'm getting one of those stupid Chihuahua shirts." She'd seen part of his collection. It was enough to make her want to migrate.

"I've got a better idea for a pair of matching ones. Custom designed, I might add. Yours will say, *I hear a voice and it doesn't like you.*"

"What about yours?"

"Mine will say, *Me either.*"

She laughed as she rolled atop him. "I like it, but I feel like I should add that the voice in my head kind of likes you."

"What of the woman?"

"She likes you, too," she murmured, rubbing her nose against his.

"That's good because I like you, too."

And the moment might have gotten really sappy if Princess hadn't taken that moment to gag beside them on the bed.

But Aria didn't mind because, in her python's embrace, she finally found what she'd been searching for—a family. A home. And a bratty dog to call her own.

*

At the click of a key in the lock, Melanie stood from the couch. Ever since she'd gotten the call about the fire at Bittech, she'd wondered, *Was Andrew in there when the bombs went off?*

At least they thought it was explosives. How else to explain the massive boom and rumble? The utter destruction of a building made to withstand hurricanes.

Is my husband dead or alive? And of most interest, had he played a part in the destruction?

Once upon a time, she would have claimed no way, not her benign husband. But now that it turned out the rumors of Bittech running an experimental underground installation were true, she realized she didn't know the man she'd been sleeping beside for years.

The bright red door, which she'd painted to stand out from the others in the cookie-cutter neighborhood, swung open, and through it stepped Andrew.

Her husband.

The traitor.

When her best friend, Renny, had called her with the news about Bittech, not just the destruction of it, but what had been discovered before it blew, she'd not wanted to believe it. Believing it meant reevaluating her entire life since high school. It meant admitting she'd made a colossal mistake in marrying Andrew.

Andrew walked in as if he still held the right. Hell no.

She raised the gun in his direction. "Don't take another step."

He barely spared her a glance. He never spared her anything, not his attention or his love. He definitely never let her borrow his nice and shiny BMW. She got stuck with the practical mini van. She enjoyed her petty revenge by sending the boys with their daddy in his pretty car—with slushies.

Tossing his keys on the side table, Andrew dropped his briefcase. He still had yet to acknowledge her or the weapon she aimed.

"I said don't move. Or, even better, get out."

That finally drew his attention. The traitor raised eyes and didn't even bother to hide his disdain. "Or you'll what, Melanie? Shoot me. We both know you don't have the guts. So stop wasting my time and pack a bag. Quickly now. Wake the boys, too, if you intend to bring them. We're leaving here as soon as our transportation arrives."

"I'm not going anywhere with you."

"I'm sorry, did I say you had a choice?" Andrew's hand shot out and grabbed hold of the wrist with the gun. He possessed a stronger, wiry strength than she would have credited. He held her with ease.

"Asshole. Let go of me. I'm not going with you."

She struck at him with her free hand, but the man she thought she knew, the one who couldn't stand the sight of blood, the one who wouldn't even squish a spider, held fast. Held her firmly. With his free hand, he slapped her.

Her head rocked to the side, and she tasted blood as the edge of her teeth cut her lip.

"Don't hit her." The low growl came from behind Andrew.

Usually, running into Wes made her massively uncomfortable, the whole ex-boyfriend thing being a large part of it. Not this time. She'd never been happier to see him.

Despite her throbbing cheek, she still turned a triumphant smile on Andrew. "Yeah, Andrew. Don't hit me."

"You meddle in things that are none of your business, gator," Andrew barked over his shoulder as Wes filled the open doorway.

"Men don't hit women."

"And employees don't back talk to their bosses. So mind your place, gator, or you won't have that cushy job anymore. I called you here to help me, not give me lip."

"Help you?" She uttered the words through frozen lips.

She waited for Wes to refute Andrew's words. To slap her bastard husband upside the head. Instead, Wes tightened his lips.

He's not here to save me. The realization hurt more than it should have.

"How could you?" she whispered.

He said the same thing to her now as he had when they'd broke up, and she'd cried, "why?"

"Because."

But Melanie wasn't a teenage girl anymore, and as she slammed her foot down on Andrew's, forcing him to loosen her gun-wielding hand, she retorted, "Because isn't an answer."

Neither was shooting first, her husband or her ex-boyfriend.

Bang. Bang. But it sure felt damned good.

The End...for now.

Be sure to check out the next story, featuring Wes and Melanie: Gator's Challenge.

Author Bio

Hello and thank you so much for reading my story. I  hope I kept you well entertained. As you might have noticed, I enjoy blending humor in to my romance. If you like my style then I have many other wicked stories that might intrigue you. Skip ahead for a sneak peek, or pay me a visit at http://www.EveLanglais.com This Canadian author and mom of three would love to hear from you so be sure to connect with me.

Facebook: http://bit.ly/faceevel
Twitter: @evelanglais
Goodreads: http://bit.ly/evelgood
Amazon: http://bit.ly/evelamz
Newsletter: http://evelanglais.com/newrelease